Talk

# The Talk of the Town

A novel - In three volumes - Vol. 1

Talk

**The Talk of the Town**
*A novel - In three volumes - Vol. 1*

ISBN/EAN: 9783337351007

Printed in Europe, USA, Canada, Australia, Japan

Cover: Foto ©Andreas Hilbeck / pixelio.de

More available books at **www.hansebooks.com**

# THE TALK OF THE TOWN.

A NOVEL.

IN THREE VOLUMES.

VOL. I.

London:
T. CAUTLEY NEWBY, PUBLISHER,
30, WELBECK STREET, CAVENDISH SQUARE,
1868.

# THE TALK OF THE TOWN.

---

## CHAPTER I.

IF you go from Daryngworth, which is a considerable place, and the terminus of a loop line off the Great Northern, to the market town of Ripplestock—when you have travelled some nine miles along the high road, you see a steep country lane branching off to the left.   Once up that, and on the top of the hill, Sawtry Marshal lies just below you.   There is a great lake, away at the other side whereof all is so still that you would doubt this land being a park.   Only the slight wreath of smoke rising out of trees, perhaps a bell rung far away, or an iron gate slamming, tells you that there is a fine house among the elms yonder. The country lane before named is a short cut to Sawtry Marshal domain, and when it has run over this hill, it joins the broad, level turnpike, which goes from a certain Chartloe village to Ripplestock. At the other side of this turnpike, the park begins.

Let anyone, thinking of the park they know best, and have the clearest picture of in their head, fancy they are looking over it now; for most people will end by imagining a story of a country place to go on in the park they remember best.

Such thorn and oak trees grew at Sawtry as all have seen on English hill sides; they were knee deep in fern on those slopes across the lake, and a long, yellow grass flourished in the park. To this common, pretty spot, must be added a lake, a mile long, and dotted with islands; for its lake made Sawtry Marshal famous.

Now a still December sky sobers all the woods, and lake, and islands into a pleasant winter's twilight. Great flocks of crows and pigeons pass, travelling home to those long brown covers and fir plantations. To watch these pigeons, you might fancy each one carrying dispatches, so earnestly do they hurry back, stuffed full of turnip tops, to their roosting trees. And there go some, with a "bag," surely, for yonder tall peak of firs. They brush the top branches, and with a high-up, mysterious sound, pass on. But it is a favourite place; with musical cooings, half a dozen pigeons flutter aloft among the branches, and, as their wings close, comes a clap and a flash. Whish! goes a charge of shot up into the middle of them; there follows the second barrel, and down come birds hitching among the branches. In the dark below, there stood a boy, and so' bright and white they huddled on the ground, that he could easily find them all. His shots, breaking on the quiet evening, made the next flock turn and dive in the air, and, avoiding that belt of wood, they vanish far away. Then, the boy who had shot (hereinafter named George) picked up his birds, and thought it made enough. It was getting late, and the light depressed him, trickling through these sombre branches "I haven't heard Berty doing much," he said, to himself. "What'll he say, I wonder, when he hears about 'Kildare?'" A dozen warm birds had to be crammed into his battered old game bag; and fingering over their full crops and plump breasts with some triumph, he came out from the firs and took his road through the damp grass and fern. Half the park was hid in a rising mist, and it was nearly dark. 'They were dressing for dinner, by all those lights in the bed-rooms,' he thought. This was a happy hour for George. No grown up, law-loving people were about, to care what he did; he could idle near the fountain in the garden, and call the golden pheasants; or sit toasting himself over the harness-room fire, listening to the stories Neal would tell him. If that failed, he should seek out Patsy Carroll, the Irish boat-man, who had charge of the lake, and hear him and his big sons talk.

Pushing open the hall door, he was in a lofty place, which had broad stone steps right and left, running up to a gallery, whence opened the great doors of the library and grander chambers. About the walls were heads and horns, birds, cases with fish, arrows and bows, and some armour. By this light they were dim and half alive. On the billiard table below sat his brother Berty, swinging his heels wildly, and recklessly sucking away at a wooden pipe. He had been out with the keeper, having leave to kill partridges and hares, while his younger brother shot only pigeons.

The keeper stood by, unscrewing a broken nipple, and Neal, the groom, had just come round to tell the squire's man that Mr. Bertram's hunter was quite lame; hence, Mr. Bertram sat kicking his heels about, his big eyes wide open in despair, and his fat white forehead squeezed into a frown.

As this was the hour of suspension of the law, little Stephen, the youngest brother, had taken possession of perilous balustrades along the gallery above. Near him stood a maid, who, by feats of skill, continued to save his life. Seeing his brother's gun, he craved alms vociferously. " Deorge, div me some powder, won't oo' ? I've dot a cannon, and keeper says I may soot. Oh ! Bertie has lots, and won't dive me any."

" Master Stephen," cried the maid, rescuing him afresh; " your mamma will be extremely displeased if you fall into the hall below, and lose your life, or are laid on a bed of sickness."

" Hold your row up there," cries Berty ; " you want to shoot all the deer with your old cannon, Tiff. What'll pa say? Elizabeth, take that young Tiff and stick him in bed. Traylen, send old Elizabeth to bed."

Traylen, the keeper, a confirmed bachelor and Yorkshireman, was Berty's great ally and flatterer.

Elizabeth retorted scornfully from her high position on the gallery.

"Easy see our pa's dressing, or we wouldn't be whiffing our fine pipes. I can put myself a bed, and little school boys, too."

"Ask maid who put t' rabbit to her bed New Year's night, Master Berty?" whispered the keeper.

But Elizabeth had just led away the suicidal Stephen.

George leant his elbow on the banisters, and munched the top of his loading rod, thinking how great a hero his eldest brother was. He could marvel at his grandeur all day long. Might not Berty take out the best setters, or even the pointers, as he liked? For him keepers should be ready at any hour to find sport or to mark. He never lacked powder and shot, or had to coax to have his gun or his spurs cleaned. And now, too, since he had been to school, he appeared in such wonderful suits, while George still wore the home-made cloth of infancy. Then boldly he spoke, and with an ease that George's confused speeches never could approach—

"Well, here, Bo," he moaned, "Kildare's lame, and of course George Musgrave meets at Chartloe cross roads to-morrow. Lord Knaresborough's keeper says there's a vixen and two cubs in Rother Spinney, and I can't go. What'll I do?"

George was very sorry. He had known all this hours ago.

"What did you shoot?"

"Oh! my! what am I to do? Why I shot two old wood pigeons and a heron ; and I wanted to shoot a lot of these old hen pheasants, only Traylen wouldn't let me. And I shot Mrs. Wright's tom cat on the school-house wall, and then we got Patsy Carroll, and got him to put up his hat for a mark."— '

Here distant doors opening announced their father's approach. All vanished save the two boys. The Squire came shuffling along the stone gallery holding a candlestick. Stopping, he threw the light on the little boys below, and after looking for a minute, broke into one of his gruff laughs—

"Who's going to hunt to-morrow, Master Berty? Fine scenting weather to-night. You go and dress. George, don't idle your brother, sir."

Berty was to be paraded in the dining-room at dessert, but George and Stephen were for early beds.

"Likely I'll go and have tea with the maids," said George to himself.   His father's speeches wounded him perpetually, and he had found out lately for himself that he and Stephen were very small powers in the house indeed.   Thinking that Mrs. Carrol would perhaps give him some of her oat cakes for supper, he strolled out into the dark again.   To his joy, Neal was there still, and George leapt up to his shoulder.

" Neal, tell me that story about the three white colts now.   Do—do, Neal."

And before many minutes George was sitting on a low box by the harness room fire, his chin on his hands, listening to Neal's solemn stories.

" Now I'll light a pipe, with your leave, Master George," said the groom.

" Oh! yes, Neal.   Do you know, I want Master Berty to have old Bess to hunt on to-morrow, as he can't ride ' Kildare.' "

" But she's at Skellingworth, to begin of, Master George.   Baxter's clipping her."

" I know that.   Why on earth couldn't Baxter come here, as he always does, I wonder ?"

" Well, sir, it were the Squire's orders.  There
were two cart colts going  to Mr. Wakely's, and
he says, ' Peter  must ride  her along ;' and the
Squire thinks Baxter's th' only man in the country can clip."

" Now," said George, " he'll have finished by
this, I know; and I'll tell you, Neal, I'll walk
over to-night and bring her back, and Master
Berty can ride her to-morrow.  No, I don't care ;
I've thought it all over."

" Well, sir," says Neal, quite over  persuaded,
" the Squire may be mighty angry. Well, Baxter
—he'll be likely drunk at this hour, too.  Well,
see Baxter's wife, Master George—she ain't so
much one of the fighting kind."

Then George left the fire, and set off  to seek
his horse.  He was little, and the night was
pitch dark.  He could not see well at first, and
the rising wind, with its weird suggestions, ab-
sorbed his thoughts. But by and bye, he reflected,
how Berty knew  nothing of this, and how proudly
he could  greet him to-morrow, before he was
up, with the news that he might hunt after all.
This ' Bess' mentioned was George's hunter, when
not arbitrarily sent off to grass. She was a great,
plain beast, of light bay colour.   In George's

hands, however, with snaffle bridles, she had done many wonders. As he tramped on, he remembered gradually that Berty would despise her ugly looks now, and that he and his horse would be scorned. But the warm hope that he might be able to give Berty some pleasure, carried him over the nine miles between the park and Baxter's cottage. The Baxter family were celebrating some feast in a dingy ale-house, whence a voice called out,—

" Who be you, wanting horses at this hour?"

" I'm Master George Claude Newmarch, of Sawtry Marshal," said the little fellow. Whereupon all the candles should have flared up, no doubt. Anyhow, Mrs Baxter came upon that, and being the most sober person of the lot, found his hunter for him.

" No, she had no saddle nor bridle," she said. He had only a halter to lead his horse by, and was afraid that some of those drunken men whom he saw inside the door might follow him. But, through mud and wind, he was back at the stables again by one o'clock in the morning. It was a long way, with each clump of trees a ghost's outpost, to a boy. But before this he had found out, "if you try, you will get any hard thing over."

"I think she looks uglier than ever, close clipped," he said, dejectedly, when he had awakened Neal from before the fire, and saw his horse by the lanthorn's light. "Stick her in some stall to-night. Good night, Neal."

He climbed in at the scullery window, and braving the rats in the lonely passages, staggered to bed at last.

Next morning George was lazy. He never liked getting out of bed, but loved instead to pull the clothes up to his ears and feel warm again. At last, however, he sauntered into his brother's room, and found him sitting up in bed, fondling his knees, a big hunting-whip by his pillow. He looked very happy, his fat face beaming under a fringe of glossy black curls. "I was thinking if we only had grand, big beds like these at Harrow," says he. "Look, we've got things that are shut up like boxes. Once, George, we had some acting, you know. I was a young lady—had to be awfully ill—and we had to smash open the top of the bed to get out one blanket to cover me."

"It's a grand scenting day, Berty," says George, trying to lead up to his piece of news.

"Ah! yes—so much the sadder," said Berty, shaking his head.

Then he went on pensively cracking his whip.

"Look! Suppose you were to hunt, after all. I want to tell you I've got a horse for you, if you won't laugh—promise. Well, then, there's Bess."

"Oh! how glorious!" cried Berty. "But she ain't here: and you'll want her."

"No—I've no tops, and I've lost my gaiters. But she ain't pretty to look at: I've got her, though."

"Oh! how stunning!" cries Berty. "I shall wear my white leathers. Pretty! We'll make her go," and he made his whip crack like a pistol.

George's fears were gone now. Berty did not remember who to thank; nor would any one, perhaps, ever know of that long walk. George's point was gained, however. So at breakfast Berty appeared in a red coat, after all; he wore his leathers, too, the unpliant creases of which he bore very patiently, sustained by pride. His father was busily talking to Henry Stacey and Sir Charles Hamby's eldest son, when he came in, and so nobody noticed him.

They were talking politics; the politics of that day, which are past galvanising now—at least, in a conversational, breakfast-table sense. There was Mr. Hamby, a rich man, with a red beard, then most rare. Henry Stacey, younger brother to the Squire of Bullingworth near here. He was intensely loyal to his own county, knowing everybody, and every horse, and most of the dogs and dumb creatures in it. There was Lord Exmoor, a well-behaved young man to look at, who cared for nothing but hunting; and there was a little man, who told anecdotes, and was full of *notabilia*. Lady Adelaide Newmarch made tea and Lady Exmoor sat by her. Already they had had two reminiscences from Mr —who shall we say? for he is still alive—Mr. Payster; but it was early, and he was still faint.—

"Payster!" (of course, that isn't his real name), called out the squire, " Charles Hamby here wants to hear that story about what Lord So-and-So said to you about fishing in the Test."

There had been no such request, but this was the squire's humour.

" Why do you ask that horrid little man to come here ? I see him everywhere one goes," said Lady Exmoor, gently, while the anecdote was in the telling.

Berty still stood unnoticed.

"How they all jaw!" said he to George. "Why does Charles Hamby wear a red beard? I hate little old Payster. Do you know, he keeps little packets of anecdotes on the table in his room —made me think of powders. Lady Exmoor's pretty."

"Now, Exmoor," said the squire, going to the window, and throwing it up, "I'll shew you how I call my deer, and feed 'em. Hulloa!" he continued, seeing Berty. "Here's a young gentleman going to hunt. Why, they said your horse was lame, sir."

Now there was a horse being ridden up and down on the gravel below.

"Drop your hands, man, and let me see that horse trot," said the squire to the groom. "Drop your hands, I say. Ho! ho! I see this is my son George's hunter. Why, here's a scalded pig, sir! Well, Master Berty, look here! you holloa as if you saw the fox, and George Musgrave is sure to come up—and buy your horse!"

"Oh! yeth," said Berty, nettled; "I don't mind. Bo set all the field at Turpin's Goss jumping a swing gate on her. And pounded a lot of the Blues, who were out that day, too."

"Quite a chemical process," said Mr. Hamby.

"She seems all muscle," he added, looking at her tail, whence nearly all the hair had receded.

I don't know which of the two boys had most pleasure that day—Berty, riding off across the park to get by a short cut through Lord Knaresborough's woods to Chartloe Cross-roads; or George, fondly watching him depart. He and Tiff spent a very happy day with Patsy Carroll, catching eels from a punt. When it was getting dark, Berty rode home. It was always the boys' custom to give a report after hunting to their father, and Berty made his way to the library, just pleasantly tired, and feeling quite a workman in his splashed leathers and tops.

"Well, sir, sold your horse?" said his father.

"Oh! no, no, papa. Very few people out. We found in Rother Spinney, of course; and went awful fast 'cross Chartloe Park to that big wood of old Stacey's—runs in a curve."—

"Purehay Walk—go on."

"Oh! yes—I never can remember that place."—

"Lost him there, I fancy?"

"Yes. There wasn't an atom of scent in cover. Then we found an old vixen in Thieves' Acre, and ran, like anything, over those big meadows, other side of the Leyn, towards Farthingstock—lots of fencing. But they changed foxes in a little go'ss above the village, and went back just the way we came; and lost him near your woods. Then they drew Chalford Purlieus, and found two cubs, and went pottering about till 'twas so late I left them."

" Was George Musgrave out?"

" No; James Musgrave was, but Lord Knaresborough did master. Old Cook staked his second horse in Purehay Walk. He asked after you. There was an old parson out, admired Bess awfully, and was telling me what horses you used to have."—

" Aye, aye—I daresay."

Mr. Newmarch had not hunted for twenty years, having quarrelled with the late master of these hounds, and with most of the subscribers; but he knew every yard of the country by heart. " So you hadn't a bad day for the woods, eh?"

" Oh! no. The hounds went awful fast once or twice, and I was carried first-rate. Why! there was one place—with an old iron gate—and Cook was breaking it down for Lady Knaresborough— and I went at it close by, and ' Bess' flew the whole thing. She gave such a scream!"

" Who ?—the horse ?   I daresay the hounds weren't running at all at the time.   Nice school-boy's trick, too.   Watts 'll tell me all about it market-day."

" There was such a jolly chesnut old Doubleday had out, and he was wanting Lady Knares-borough to buy it.   So she said, ' Oh ! we must wait and see how we come off after Lincoln spring, Mr. Doubleday.'   Fancy !"

" Pooh ! give me my candle."

George had sat all this time on a stool by the window unnoticed. "And," said his father, taking a survey of him, "you're going to school, sir. D'you hear that."

His heart swelled in his little breast.   He could have choked.

" Hurrah !" cried Berty, when they were alone. " Why, you'll be in the same house with me : it's just as good fun as being at home—in summer."

George only shook his head.

" Why, we had a fellow ran away from home to get back, once—Bovin Minor.   He wouldn't stay at home, all they could do."

" But I'll be sent to some utter private school," George said.   He had picked that up from Berty already.  "And all those beagles just coming on !"

George had a pack—of one very old beagle and two round puppies, who used to try, when let loose, to feed on the old beagle.   These were his pride and joy.   He could only be consoled by hearing full details of the day's hunting, lying on his back in the dark upstairs.

According to custom, Berty was summoned that evening to dessert.   He was a shy boy ; for these were days before boys of fifteen kept broughams, and belonged to the Raleigh.   He was afraid of company therefore.   What he most admired among the grown up people was Lady Exmoor, who sat there all radiant with loveliness, and not saying a word.   To be worshipped, one would think.   But people got used to her, doubtless, seeing her day after day.   My lord seemed to have done so, at all events.   Berty longed to go and stand by her, but was afraid.   After a while he saw her raise her great eyes—fortunately she did so seldom—then he could not look at her at all.   He was between Charles Hamby and his father.

"Where's little Guy Faux, to-night?" asked the  former gentleman : he meant George, with whom he had made great friends. And George would rather hear him talk than anything else in the world, and by looking up at the corners of his eyes used to know when he was laughing at people, which they did not, perhaps.

"Think I might go over there, papa?" whispered Berty, looking towards Lady Exmoor. "Might I, I wonder?"

But then his courage failed, and no one had heard him but Mr. Hamby. That endless discussion was going on about a man trespassing in one's park, in order to gather mushrooms say— the difficulty of removing him without committing an assault, and the puzzle that it was generally.

"So they went by my woods without drawing 'em, to-day, Exmoor," said the squire. "Cook hates my keeper, I know."

"Traylen's too fond of his pheasants," my lord observed. "Which do you like best, shooting or hunting, youngster?" said Charles Hamby to Berty.

"I think I can tell for him," Lord Exmoor answered.

But Berty thought he ought to stand up in Traylen's defence first.

"We've got a fox in Clerken Wood. I've seen him," said he.

Charles Hamby grinned. "Well, now you've got much better taste than Exmoor has—I can see that. You take your gun and go out early to-morrow, and shoot that fox, my boy."

"Perhaps it's done already," suggested Lord Exmoor.

"Done already? Not bad. That reminds me of—" began Mr. Payster, who had been again impressing on Charles Hamby the difficulty he and some great man had found in fishing the Test, without a floss line—"reminds me of a story they used to tell of old Sir John Lintstock and his nephew, at Gibraltar. Old gentleman at breakfast one day—and says he, 'Frank, my boy, I think that fellow looked rather queerly across the table at you, last night, at mess. Ought to take some notice.' 'Ah! yes, sir,' says the youngster, ' I shot him at daybreak, this morning,' " &c., &c.

"Now I'm a Radical, Hamby," said the squire, "have been since '29. I'm going to send those two—two young fellows you've seen about—to Eton. Lots of equality there. Got to make their way — make friends. This youngster here, he's at Harrow. I was a Radical there, as long ago as Drury's time—barred him out. Well, we were all there, since my grandfather. And now, see how the world's improved. There's my lord Knaresborough—he was at that same school, and his father. Yes, by Gad! I was the old fellow's fag—and he goes and sends his eldest boy to Eton. Grander place, they tell me."

This was a favourite sneer of Mr. Newmarch's. He was so eccentric a politician, and so un-accommodating a neighbour in many ways, that he and most of the county families were on the worst of terms. With Lord Knaresborough there was, perhaps, naturally a soreness. The reigning Earl could barely even be civil to Brian New-march. They never met at Newmarket, which was his Lordship's place of business, and there was little between these old neighbours, even though their covers grew into each other. Barton Stacey, of Bullingworth, and the squire were deadly foes in politics, and their wives,—who prayed for each other's conversion to a better frame of mind,—were estranged on matters of doctrine. At Monksylver, there was a Mr. Basledon, who was mad; and their next nearest neighbour, Miss Bezant, at Otonbury, had married her coachman. So, but for a few old friends who still came, and put up with the Squire's odd ways and tempers, Sawtry would have been quite deserted.

# CHAPTER II.

BEFORE many days little George had laughed away and almost forgotten the great event that was impending over him. Often now he was in heroic Berty's room, before the other was up. Every saying of Berty's was so brilliant and memorable since he had been to school. It must, after all be a wonderful place, where one got such an air—indescribable, yet most admirable. He determined to take an opinion about it all ; for Berty's accounts, when he sought details, were sometimes disconnected or mythical. After the grown-up breakfast was over, George strayed about quietly from room to room till he got to the library. He had an idea that his father was not here, but sitting in the garden. And so he was, beyond the foun-tain, under his favourite tree, flirting disgracefully with Lady Exmoor. She had just brought him a light for his cigar. The old man, with his long cynical face and gaunt figure, leaning his hands on his stick, and waited on by that beautiful woman, made a queer picture.—

"Thank you, milady," said he. "Your grandmother was the first woman I ever kissed; so give me a kiss now."

"My husband is looking, you desperate man," said she, kissing his wrinkled forehead.

"Exmoor," shouted the squire, "look what your fine wife has done."

Meanwhile George had softly entered the library. There was papa's great chair, with the leather cushions in it, his thick gloves and his silk handkerchief lying on the table, classic objects for George. But nobody, save Mr. Hamby was visible. He was reading the newspaper. "Well, little conspirator," said he, "who are you going to dethrone now?"

After a pause, George asked,

"What sort of a place is Eton to be at, Mr. Hamby?"

"So you're going, eh? I wish I were you. Ah! me, yes. The first time I ever saw your papa was at Eton. I was carrying a kettle for the fellow that I was fag to, down to the river to get water for his breakfast. I was such a little chap, and my fingers so numbed, I couldn't break the ice, for 'twas in January, wasn't it? Yes. Your papa came up and filled my kettle for me. Wasn't I glad. How would you like all that?"

George knit his brows in thought.

"I don't think I'd mind," he said. "I suppose I'd get warm running back."

"Well, yes. Your papa smashed the ice and filled my kettle for me. He and your Uncle Felton, who was a gay young guardsman then. They had walked down from Eton. I was nearly crying with cold, I remember."

George reflected deeply on the story.

"I wouldn't mind if people saw me bear it," he thought.

"Good-by, now, little man," said his friend. "I must finish my comic paper—all abusing me. So you won't give in, if your paws are ever so cold, eh?" And he was soon buried in the attack on himself.

George left, full of importance after his conference with his friend, who, he had a sort of idea, was above all education or schools. Then he sought Berty at the stables. "Let us have one more day with the beagles," said he. " I may be going away for years soon."

Berty was in a superbly lazy mood, sitting on a bucket and playing with a setter pup. "Oh! bother !" said he, and turned the pup head-over-heels. " There ! the brute's bit me."

" I'll let you have my horn all the time, if you'll come," said George.

" Oh ! well—don't make a row. What does papa say ?"

" You go and ask him—it's no use me," said poor George.

Berty went.

" May we have horses out, sir," said he, " For the beagles ?"

" Beagles, eh ? Yes. Eat up all I've got I know. Go 'long, if you like," said the Squire. So they had ' Kildare ' and ' Bess ' saddled.

" May I come ?" says Stephen, who had tracked them after escaping, no doubt, from Elizabeth's clutches. " I have a pony."

" Oh ! here's this awful Tiff," says Berty ; " send him away."

" You musn't come here, sir ; we're going to Daryngworth to buy scythes that would cut your legs."

Tiff stood gazing at them with his grey eyes wide open, and his frizzy light hair all on end—a quaint little man.

"Is Master Stephen to have a pony, sir?" says Neal.

"Good heavens, Neal! I don't know. Ask the squire," lisped Berty, in a rage.

Then George sought his beloved hounds. Out they rolled frantically on the top of each other, while George—who fondly fancied that they knew their names—holloaed to each in turn, and Berty blew his horn heroically. They drew a couple of big hedges on the Bullingworth-road, and finding a rabbit, had one very "good thing" from one side of the road to the other—into a drain. This took them some time, and they were joined by a white terrier from the village. Berty thought that *infra dig*.

"It's not such a bad dog," said George; "we may as well allow it to hunt." Berty continued to blow his horn.

Then they 'drew' up the hill outside the park palings, and got on the scent of a rabbit in the open field, which they ran on to Mr. Stacey's land, and lost by the rectory wall. They drew up the boundary of the park once more and killed a rabbit in a plantation. This was very exciting. Kildare refused every fence he was put at, and Berty sat on the horse, laughing and blowing his horn all the faster. A strange, fat little figure, on the great hunter.

George, riding furiously to be with his hounds, sent old Bess over the biggest places, whether it was called for or not, and was soon muddy up to the eyes.

" I've had enough of this, Bo," sang out Berty to George, who was now trying for the scent with ' Barmaid ' in another field.

" It's no go, I suppose," George answered, lurching ' Bess ' over a gap, stopped with a big rail, back into the field where his brother was. " But I wouldn't let old ' Kildare ' have his own way," he continued; " kick him over that hedge into the road; look out you don't land on the drain."

Berty puckered up his little Cupid mouth, hit Kildare across the head with George's pet hunting-horn, and sent him as hard as he could down the hill. The horse shook his great neck, snapped at the cheek of the bit, and seeing the broad growing hedge in front of him, reared up and spun round from it as quick as thought. Berty clung to him like a spider, enjoying George's disgust, and knocked and knocked the precious horn about his horse's violent ears.

"'Kildare's' only fresh," he said. "Quite right; he don't want to jump—with a lot of old beagles."

This was more than George could stand. "Let me get on him," said he, doggedly.

Berty jumped off.

"Oh! you brute! Ah! you brute!" says George, growling from his seat on Kildare's back. He took the horse a canter up the field, scolding at him thus, and a scowl on his face; then wheeled him sharp round, lay back in the saddle, stuck in his heels, and with a shout, jammed 'Kildare' at the place. The horse slid fifteen feet on the slippery grass, half stopped, and jumped some five feet high, over into the road.

Berty came through the gate with good-tempered Bess, and George said nothing; but triumphed, doubtless, in his heart.

"Hulloa! here's the carriage coming," Berty cried; and the Sawtry horses were made out through the haze, spinning towards them.

"Where can they have been? calling for parcels or for fish at the Railway Station, I think," said

George, still breathless. " Why, there's a girl—
oh! who can that be?"

" 'Twas a new maid," says Berty.

" Not it," George answered, " For Pringle was
sitting up stiff with her back to the horses. And
the small one in the good seat." He knew by
experience how these things went.

" Oh! bother!" cried Berty, " Now I know. If
it's our cousin, she'll be wanting to go about with
us. I hate girls—all brutes!" Then he thought
of Lady Exmoor—she must, by the way, have
been a girl once, he recollected.

When back in the house,—before they could
hide upstairs,—their mother sent for them to her
sitting-room, where was the Squire reading a
letter, and good-natured Pringle warming a little
girl's hands—a tall, slight child, and very pale—
such as young heroines are.

" Make friends with your cousin, Bertram,"
said Lady Adelaide ; " and you, George,
dearest."

The little girl gave them a cold hand.

" Kiss your cousin, Master Bertram dear," said
Mrs. Pringle.

She meekly held her head still and Berty, with
a sulky look, went up and bobbed his mouth

against her cold cheek ; while she dutifully made
the sound of a small kiss.  Then he withdrew to
stare out of the window.

"I saw these before, Aunt Adelaide," the
child said, in a plaintive voice.  "He jumped
near us on a brown horse."

"Eh !" says the Squire, "where was that?"

"Opposite old Mrs. Slowly's cottage, sir,"
explained Pringle.  "Mr. Bertram jumped the
hedge upon his horse, sir."

"That's a big jump, Master Berty," says his
father.

"What!" says Berty, whisking round when
his own name caught him.

"You pay attention to what I say, young
gentleman," grumbled the Squire, "though you
can ride over a fence."

Berty could not make out what on earth they
were at, and catching George's eye, shrugged his
shoulders contemptuously.  As for the younger
brother, he was too proud to say a word, but
thought bitterly how the credit had gone to the
wrong person.  "Perhaps," he consoled himself,
"I'm like Berty when it's a little dark."

As soon as they were free they ran up to the
nursery, and Berty rolled on the bed, muddy

boots and all. The firelight made great shadows over the room, and George and Stephen sat on the hearth-rug, toasting their faces.

"I wish I could make rabbits with my fingers, like Charles Hamby," said George.

Tiff climbed upon his shoulders. "Bo, what is our cousin like?"

"Oh! I think she's not bad," whispered George. He was afraid of being heard by the still sulky Berty, who, by prerogative, fashioned the complexion of thought in the nursery. His opinion was unfavourable. There was no appeal. "Mrs. Wright, get us tea," says he; "I have to dress for dinner." And while he yawned and kicked his heels, the new cousin strayed into the room.

Then the three brothers gathered in front of the fire, very shy, and keeping her in the middle of the carpet.

"I came to see Mrs. Wright," she said.

"She'll come soon, little cousin," Stephen answered.

"Do you play here?" she asked gently, gazing round the strange room.

"We don't play with girls," said Emperor Berty, and beginning to sing.

The young lady was silenced, and stood patiently by herself some way off, her white frock lit up by the firelight, and her hands primly joined in front of her. She glanced now and then at Bertie.

" I have some toys," said George, "which I'll show you."

But she did not care for his friendship, and thought it strange that the nice one would not speak to her.. He was whistling harder than ever.

" Shall I bring her all my string to play with," whispered Tiff, in George's ear.

The other, however, sadly shook his head. Of course she liked *him* best.

By and bye Berty got up. "What are you thinking of, cousin?" he asked, patronisingly.

"I am thinking," she said, simply, "of when I shall grow up and go to be presented 'at court.'"

" Pooh ! your neck is too long to be shewn to the Queen ; we think you are very ugly !"

Then Pringle, Lady Adelaide's maid, came and took her away.

" Mrs. Pringle, have I a long neck ?" asked Helen Mallorie ; and she felt it thoughtfully with her fingers for some time.

"To be sure not, Miss Mallorie; you're only lonesome, miss, for the first time with strangers, but you'll be very happy with milady," said the servant, and petted her as much as she was able with tea and famous toast; then helped her to undress after the long day she had had.

"What prayers do you say, dear?" asked the servant.

The little Helen, in her long night dress, knelt with bare feet at the good tempered woman's lap and prayed.

"God bless mamma, little brothers, and nurse. Teach me to be a good girl and keep me from all sinful thoughts, words, and deeds, morning and evening. Take care of me when I go to sleep, and forgive me trespasses as I forgive, for—"

"Say 'God bless uncle, and aunt, and cousins', now," interrupted Mrs. Pringle, gently.

"God bless Bertram, Lady Adelaide Newmarch. The dark one too; amen."

Pringle laughed.

"Not quite right, miss;" but the child was nearly asleep.

*    *    *    *    *

When Lady Adelaide and her husband were left alone, she sat in her arm-chair, shading her face from the fire; she yawned a little, and sighed. "It makes me young again to see that poor child, Brian," she said, doubting what impression all this had made on her husband. " She is like her mother, Edmund's steward writes to me, but not so beautiful as that family, I am sure, and none of their firmness apparently. What a life is my brother's!"

" Well, I don't know—that may be, milady. I'm very proud to be of use to your family, and it's a fine thing to have one's brother-in-law a Banker, too. Your sister's husband's Bank writes to me this morning—'Sir,—We have the honour to inform you your account is now overdrawn two hundred and seventeen pounds nine shillings. We are, your obedient servants, Wynn Ellis,' and so on. So I wrote back—'Gentlemen—I have the honour to acknowledge your letter, and I have this day drawn a cheque on you for eighteen hundred and twelve pounds odd. I am your obedient servant, Brian Newmarch.' Why don't Charles Ellis come down here, milady? I want him to sing in my church again. He'll only sing to your sister; sang her poor heart away long ago. They tell me he's growing as old as I am, too. Is my Lord Newbury going to be married now?"

" Ah! Brian. Hush!"

By Newbury, Lady Adelaide meant her brother, Earl of Newbury, Viscount Andleby, Baron Orville, and so forth. The Earl was a widower, without children; an eccentric man. His three sisters, however, reflected the qualities of their admirable grand parent Evelina, Lady Orville, whose woes, temptations, and final happiness, are well known in story. Lady Adelaide we have met. Blanche, the eldest, had, when a girl, made a starvation match with Charles Ellis, who was then a most charming dancer. They had gone to live in lodgings, and for some years presented a great warning to the reckless, till Charles Ellis was taken into his cousin's Bank. He was now old, and he had forgotten how to dance; and was, indeed, the Bank himself, all other Wynns and Ellis's having decreased out of this world. Lady Penelope, the youngest, had become the wife of that Arthur Felton, of the Foot Guards, who stood by when Mr. Charles Hamby had tried to fill his kettle from the frozen Thames.

The Earl of Newbury had married a beautiful

woman, who died within a few months. He had his own story and romance. At Andleby there is a picture of Fanny Countess of Newbury, lovelier than could be originated by any artist. That, however, is the Earl's matter. No one in his county had seen him for twenty years, and they said strange things of him.

His Countess, who died, had a sister. Her fate was to marry a young curate for love; and together this couple lived on nothing ever after. In a year, or less perhaps, they had a daughter, who was the little Helen Mallorie. So poor had they been that Lord Newbury, trotting one Wednesday by the side of the then premier, from Croxton Park to Sproxton Thorns, had begged of him a chaplaincy for Mr. Mallorie; and the foolish couple were quickly shipped off to Calcutta—there to follow each other to the grave within a year, leaving little Helen behind, sometimes to be with Mr. Bowes, the land steward, at Andleby, sometimes at Rushworth, with Lady Penelope Felton. Now she had come to her Aunt Adelaide. At one time the Earl had taken pleasure in having this child brought to him to look at; but latterly, he was a terrible invalid at times, few people saw him, and his little relative seemed to be quite forgotten.

Mr. Newmarch said, "Is this little blowsy thing to have teachers, milady? They tell me they ought to learn."

"I suppose she is quite ignorant, poor orphan; she never knew a mother's care. Poor Edmund was her only friend, and who can say that he will ever see her again?"—"And a pretty fair friend to have, too," the husband remarked.—"Scripture," Lady Adelaide continued, "tells us that the wind is ever tempered to the shorn lamb, Brian."

"Mighty bad farming they must have had there," he growled — clasping his knees and rocking to and fro in his chair before the fire—"Now who ever heard of shearing a lamb, I'd like to know?"

"Oh! Brian, Brian, remember whose words those are that you mock at."

"Well! I ain't laughing at your holy things. 'Twas Sterne that wrote it, they tell me; but I don't know. And so there ain't any chance of an heir to my lord, or that Blanche won't be a Countess, eh? Well, I think so, too. And Charles Ellis's boy is safe to have Andleby and all the Vale of Weopham to live in. Well! well!—I remember when them two were married first, and lived in Great Coram Street over a doctor's shop!"

## CHAPTER III.

THE little girl who thus came for shelter did not give her mysogonist cousins much trouble. She lived in submission, with Pringle and Lady Adelaide. The mornings were spent in milady's boudoir, learning some lessons. At times Berty came there to listen to a Psalm being read, or to promise to learn a hymn by next time. He was very nice when he was obliged to sit quiet, and Helen could look at him. If he would only be always good and gentle like that! There was never a meeker pupil known than she herself. No chapter was too long or hymn too intricate for her to listen to, without frowning or wanting to yawn; and of those things milady thought there could not be too much.

Thus the time went on very peacefully. Many things at Sawtry always remained strange to

Helen. Without Mrs. Pringle, she hardly cared to venture beyond the garden or the walk to church, which church, indeed, stood somewhere between the stables and the kitchen garden; she would not go even down to the lake alone, and most things were dangerous. The deer especially had to be avoided, for their long horns were terrible; and a cow, to Helen's eyes, looked revengeful even at a distance. The days when she was very little, she had spent at Andleby, where there was no one but Mr. Bowes, the earl's land steward, and his sister—who was very deaf and kept house for him. Thus she had grown up—a silent little mortal, all alone in that great big barrack on the top of Andleby Hill. From month to month there used to be no new face to look at, and the only gala days she had ever known were when the hounds drew Hoseby Gorse at the foot of the park, and ran across before the house—once or twice in winter.

Lady Adelaide took a liking of her own to the little Helen. Fancy educational schemes were a hobby of hers; sometimes she tried such on the school children at Sawtry; sometimes in her own nursery, and here was a field ripe for any experiment. The child could be moulded as one wished, and any pet fancy of hers that she had thought of, perhaps, for her boys, could be carried out as one desired with her adopted daughter. She determined the child should be brought up perfectly; for from unbridled affections or other causes so few children really were.

Early in the new year the time came for the boys to leave home. That was a sad day for the three—their last together. The morning, to be sure, was happily spent with rats. The village scoundrel, all mud, beer, and bad language, had come over from Bullingworth with a lot of rough terriers; and Traylen and some of his men having dug up the ground in the pheasantry, hundreds of rats, young and old, were slain. This kept thought away till the boys' dinner hour. After that the three made a tour of the stables, the boat house, the dairy, and Patsy Carrol's cottage. George was indeed sad and subdued. If he had not dreaded contempt, he would have confided his sorrow to Neal, but the manly course was to say nothing. Parting with the beagles was very bitter, and he lingered after the others by the kennel. "What will become of them, now?" he murmured; and while he stood and sighed he saw Helen and Mrs. Pringle coming from the gate lodge, walking smartly.

"Well, Master George, you're going to leave us, I fear. Great change to be sure, sir."

"Oh! I don't mind a bit," said he, ruefully, looking at Helen—who had a pretty colour after their quick pace through the frosty air—and reflecting whether he had anything suitable to give her as a parting gift.

Up came Berty and Stephen. "You haven't looked at Rosamond and her foal," said they.

"Fancy forgetting that! Will you come, cousin?" said George, now softened by affliction.

"Is it ladylike?" she answered.

Pringle said, "Oh! yes, if they did not wet their shoes."

In a paddock was Rosamond, up to her girth in straw, and looking very matronly. Stephen producing some carrots, she and her little yellow foal came and munched them. Helen thought it was a dear, and not at all shy.

"I'm going to take it to school with me," said Berty.

"Will he take it?" asked Helen of Mrs. Pringle.

"No, dear; master Berty is only in fun."

"Its mamma would be sorry to part with it," said Helen.

"Pooh! she's got no sorrow," quoth he. "Are you sorry I'm going to Harrow?"

"Yes," said she, politely.

"Will you give me a kiss, then?"

Since no wise person advised her this time, "no, sir," she answered, indignantly.

"Well, kiss the filly," said Berty.

"I shall if I like."

"Tiff, fetch t' foal," he shouted.

And Tiff, catching hold of the mane, quietly kept its head against a bar, while Helen gave its little nose a kiss. Foal sneezed and shook its head, and Helen ran laughing out of the yard.

Helen was much by herself for many a day after this. By and bye she grew tall with the young trees, and Sawtry became a familiar home to her. When the boys came from school for the holidays, they were tolerably friendly, and looked on her as a crotchet of their mother's, which concerned nobody else much. Sometimes Helen had a governess—who came for a few months at a time, and did all Lady Adelaide's letter writing for her. If little guile crept into that placid life, there was little variety in it either.

Pringle's society was Helen's nearest approach to gaiety. The two would have their little jokes together, but only after Pringle's work was done for the day. Hence Helen had to construct a theory of the outer world from very remote data indeed. But, as years went on, she continued to grow up—very beautifully taught.

At school, George and Stephen "got liked" very well. George was never in trouble with Dr. Hawtrey either, never once swished; though Stephen often got sent up for absence of mind and nonchalant transgressions. George's happiest time was the football half, and it was then his school days ended suddenly, playing at the wall.

That Eton boy, who wrote to the paper—
" *Dear Bell, can you tell, what the —— is knurr and spell?*" is unnamed, like the inventor of the plough. He has never been answered. Perhaps it was George who indited that passionate poetic wail, in some back parlour of the 'Christopher;' but I doubt if his day were contemporary with the rhyme.

To the outer world the 'game at the wall' is a term of much mystery also; it was George's passion, however. It showed a fellow's pluck, he

used to believe, and he would go in and do anything, so long as there were people to look at
him. Accordingly, he was playing for his house
one day. It was supposed to be the champion
house there, and he was about the smallest boy
that had ever played in the house eleven; but he
had long since shown himself far too good to be
left out. It was two shies all.

George thought his life depended on how he
worked; a sort of fury seemed to take possession of him then, till in the middle of a tremendous 'hot' he missed his kick at the ball—
Danvers major kicked at the same time—their
legs crossed somehow, and down went George.
He was pulled out of the tussle, and laid against
the wall—very pale, with his leg broken below the
knee.

His uncle Ellis came from London that night,
and as it was late in December, those holidays
were spent by George in pain and fever, alone in
his tutor's house. Just when everyone was coming back there again, poor George bid the place
a long good-bye, and the rest of the winter found
him almost a prisoner in his little top room at
Sawtry. There were the garden trees just visible
from his bed, and many a winter sunrise found

him restless and awake, staring over the topmost branches up the yellow slope of the park. Eastward, above Clerken wood, he often watched for the sunlight coming through the frosty haze—dull bars of red scored across by the naked branches. Then he would shiver, turning from side to side—and remember Bertie and Stephen—now sleeping strong and well, and luckier than he. It had been in doubt for some time, whether his leg should not be cut off. But Lady Blanche brought the greatest surgeons down to Etou to look at him, and they let it be, after all. The pain, though, wore him away to nothing, and all his spirits went; yet never was there a pluckier patient.

Lady Adelaide came often to sit with him, bringing readings of her own; and Helen, frightened at all the bandages, used to come and ask how he was, as soon as he could sit up. Bye and bye he heard that Aunt Penelope was to have Helen at Rushworth. Lady Adelaide, to be sure, thought her brother-in-law Felton's house a very stronghold of Satan. But it was Newbury's wish that the girl should go there. Milady had done her duty by her while she was allowed.

With summer, George, thinking he would

never get well, got well again. After a time he could be wheeled down into the garden. His mother was with him more and more every day, and his father even came gradually to admire his fortitude after his own fashion. "What did you go and let a brat of a boy break your leg for, Master George?" he said, one day, finding him resting in the sun.

George shrugged his shoulders. "Why, sir, he was six feet high. Why he ran away and enlisted in the Blues once, and his people never found him, till his cousin, who's an officer in 'em, was going about the barracks, and heard him swearing like smoke, you know. They were locking him up; he was drunk—awful chap for beer—and his cousin knew him at once by his peculiar language. Then they bought his discharge. That's the story, sir."

The squire opened his eyes.—"You read that fable in some of your books—Aristophanes, I should say, Master George."

After a while it was rather jolly being an invalid. Everything was done for him, and he had to conform to no rules. He could lie in bed as long as he liked; thither Mrs. Pringle would bring him his breakfast, and no one asked how he passed his time. Then he read all the novels low down on the library shelves, and afterwards would persuade Helen to climb and fetch him those higher up. Sometimes he read farriery, sometimes The Fathers, sometimes Monte Christo and Company, or he would get Helen to read to him out of the Bible what he liked best—how the old Jews fought and slaughtered their enemies. Or the magical things in Revelations. She would scull him about on the lake as best she could, too, in the days before she had to leave for Rushworth; and then they used to discuss their projects, and what they would do if they had Sawtry of their own.

Gradually George could limp about everywhere again. It was all very well to be interesting and pitied, but he came to think he would never be quite well, and never hunt any more. Once his father had said he would only do for the church now; and, indeed, there was the living of Sawtry which fell vacant just at that time, and was in the Squire's gift.

Mr. Curry, the curate at Chartloe, was put into it, and George's name was inserted in the Bond of Resignation forthwith.

When the shooting season came, George began to think everyone was born more fortunate than he. He used to try to keep his place in line, often in great pain ; and if he missed a partridge, it made him angry and irritable for the day. There was never so jealous a shot as he now. In cover he would knock over rabbits well enough, or the swiftest 'rocketer' that ever went across in windy weather, but any one could beat him in September.

To make things worse, there was soon no one to go about with him at all ; for Helen went away to her aunt, at Rushworth, almost as soon as he could walk.

"That's a quaint little maid," said the Squire, of her. "She has hardly a word to say all day, and I don't believes she cares a button for you or anybody else, milady."

## CHAPTER IV.

ALL the same Helen Mallorie had driven off from Sawtry, sobbing, good Pringle rubbing the tears away from her cheeks. A succession of vague and immense things followed, and she found herself in the hall of a great dingy house in Cavendish Square, arrested amidst corded boxes and heaped-up trunks.

Before the coachman and Mr. Felton's other men, the good-hearted Pringle felt it due to the house to keep up her dignity, but it was hard to leave her child alone.

In a dingy back room, where the carpet had been rolled up, sat Mr. Felton, writing letters. There was luncheon still on the corner of a sideboard, while all the furniture wore white calico covers.

" Well, little girl, so you've to go down with

me. Never been in this big place before;—hum —hum." And he wrote away, leaving Helen gazing at the sallow family portraits round the room, trying to guess which of them was meant for him, and wondering whether he would turn out in his ways most like George, Traylen, or Mr. Curry, the rector. She saw with wonder the glossy blackness of his eyebrows, whiskers, and moustache, and he had very red cheeks; yet looked quite old, and his long neck was wrapped in a great satin stock and high shirt collar. By and bye he got up, and forgetting Helen, began to shift his hair in a strange way before the glass, smirking also and showing his white teeth; but seeing Helen's little face at last reflected from the corner where she was posted, he turned suddenly to her. " Now, little girl, let me see. We've got a journey yet. There's Priscilla and Dorothy at Mivart's to pay one's respects to. Shall I take this child ? Yes."

So they walked, in the close autumn evening, across Cavendish Square, down Hollis Street, coming out on the din of Oxford Street. To Helen, the brilliant confusion was like a dream of many story books. By a miracle, apparently, they did get across the broad street, then turned down a quieter one; turned off again, and stopped at last at a big hotel with open doors.

Evidently something had happened, Helen thought, from the quick way every one had of speaking and going about, in this wonderful town. She could barely understand what people said. Going upstairs, they came into a grand room, where sat two ugly little old ladies, all laces and satin and yellow skin. By them was a very pale young man.

'These cannot be his wives,' Helen thought.

"Oh! brother," they said, with sickly smiles, "how very good of you to find us out; and we have actually persuaded Arthur Maxwell to go to Lady MacPluto's very last Wednesday reading with us. The Bishop is to be there, and Arthur will like it, we are sure, though he is only in town for a minute. We have been fearing that he will find England *triste* and unattractive after the brilliant wordliness of Frascati."

They went on, hardly noticing Helen, and making pretty speeches, all in praise of the young man, who looked at nobody. Helen the while sat by the window, very lonely and wretched.

"'Pon my honour, sisters," said Mr. Felton, "I had a lot of commissions to ask you to do, and I've lost them all. They were for Lady Penelope Felton," he went on in his pompous way. "Well, Arthur, I suppose we've nothing to say to each other. You go abroad again when you said."

Arthur Maxwell was glancing wearily at Helen out of his great mournful eyes, and the child thought how pallid and interesting he looked with his long black hair. "He must be a poet," she said to herself. And indeed he was, as more than one publisher knew to their cost. "A most interesting child, sir," he murmured. "Is this a relative? I shall pray you to tell me the story another day."

"Eh? yes; Newbury's niece. Look up the Gautby's in Paris, Arthur, when you get there. You ought to have a card for Neuilly this winter, 'pon my word—if that minister friend of yours keeps his head on his shoulders—eh? Avoid those evenings at William Randolph's, if you take my advice. But there'll be no high whist, I daresay, till our best men go over after the 'Houghton.' Sisters," he said, "I'm afraid I can't tear you away from your Exeter Hall friends —I wish I were as fond of those good and charm-ing things."

Shortly afterwards they left. As the harvest moon was rising, Mr. Felton and Helen drove along Rushworth Avenue. So closed a day of wonder for Helen.

When a strange maid attended the little girl to bed, she wept to Mrs. Pringle's memory for some seconds of time, and Lady Penelope, coming with candle in hand to look at her asleep, saw how the light made crystals of the tears still wet on her cheeks.

" Just such an unlucky face as Anne Newbury had," says she.

Rushworth was a sheltered southern park, and the trees were bigger and more clothed with leaves, and the grass richer than at Sawtry. There was a larger garden, too—with mazy walks and alleys in it, where one might lose oneself easily. Mr. Felton was a person gifted with a genteel taste for the polite arts, and abroad had managed to gather together a rich collection of indifferent statues ; these, with a few ruined pillars, were set up here and there in the shrubberies, while on some of the large tree trunks might be seen displayed little marble tablets on which were engraved classic epigrams, of Mr. Felton's own making, in very wry Latin. There was a temple to fraternal piety, too, at one end of the garden,

but it was generally locked, and held nothing
but potatoes in those days.  Here, with the
young Feltons, Helen spent the  summer, not
very happily.  The children were long strangers
to each other.  Mr. Felton had been married
t wice.  The first had been a runaway match, with
an heiress, who brought this fine park of Rushworth to him—without any stupid burden of
s ettlements—and dying, left him one daughter,
Lucy.  By his second marriage with Lady Penelope, he had a son and daughter.  Lucy was
always reading good books.  As for Catherine,
the youngest, Helen thought her a silly girl,
always devising jokes and giggling.  To be sure
she had paraded her dresses and precious things
for Helen's admiration and amusement; but
these only contrasted disagreeably with the latter's own small stock.  Helen was jealous, because
there was nobody, after all, to give her nice things.
When Mr. Felton happened to come across her,
he would, to be sure, make her gallant speeches
still—ask her where she bought her rouge, and
talk about painting the lily, but no pretty pre-
sents came of it.  Lady Penelope was not
visible, except in her room.  Though really
many years younger—she was a far older looking woman than Lady Adelaide, and probably

at all times was the worst dressed person in
England; a great invalid besides, whenever
Mr. Felton was at home. Long prior to this
she had felt it her duty to separate altogether
from his world; and at certain times, if there
were a chance of any of her husband's set
coming to Rushworth, would refuse flatly to
appear at all, taking permanently to her bed,
from whence she ruled the affairs of the village, and kept up an active intercourse with
the religious world. To her many have attributed
that famous series of letters to a quarrelsome
divine which provoked the wrath and the retorts
of Bishops, periodicals, and churchmen, in
their day. Seven maids waited upon Lady
Penelope, in her own wing of the house.
Besides these, one of the children was generally
told off to attend on her each day.

Helen's turn came after a while, and there she
found Lady Penelope—in bed, a blazing fire burning in the grate, and the room looking a compound of a bookstall and a chemist's shop. Helen
in much fear and trembling, had to read a Psalm
aloud, and then appeared the cook, and stood by
the bed courtseying.

"Please miss," said she, beckoning Helen
into the outer room, "you've to write the dinner

hout hexact," and the little girl, with a great deal of help, managed that. " Please, miss, you're to submit it to milady."

Very cross she was, sending patient Helen for fifty different things, and scolding her if she could not guess all about them at once; till Helen wondered how often all this was to be looked forward to. The Lady Penelope always communicated by letter with her husband, and Helen had to write two or three notes to him before she was dismissed. One of these requested that Lady Penelope Felton might be told what guests were coming to shoot this present November. Mr. Felton returned his compliments, and Lord Hounslow, Colonel Spencer Parneys, Sir George Buskin, and Major Tiptoe meant to be good enough to give him their company.

Lady Penelope received that answer, groaning.

"I shall not see them, girl!" she said, and while Helen sat trembling by her, she went on muttering, "Hounslow! the greatest profligate in Great Britain. Spencer Parneys! disgraceful reprobate, and at his age too! The others the mere creatures of the naked and shameless ballet. Ever the same!" and so her temper was none the better.

"Well, Mrs. Weeks," says the butler, to a maid on duty outside the door. "Who's sufferin' mawt'dom, to-day?"

"Hoh! Mr. Blacker, I'm ashamed to laugh; it's that pore horfin child as come here latterly," said the maid.

"Well, Weeks, there'll be a battle royal yet, I say. She hain't been to dinner now for three months. He don't care, though; the sisters always takes his part too, I understand."

Lady Penelope had one son, as I have said, and him she would pet and quarrel with by turns, whenever he was at home from Eton. His father looked scornfully upon him, as if some dull caprice of nature had sent him such a boy. For Willie Felton took no pleasure in shooting or hunting, did not know Ascot from Oscot, and when he got on a hunter one day, to please his father, wearied of the whole thing. The boy's pleasure was in black letter volumes, in books of architecture or early art, and above all, in the romance of the saints' lives. Rumours of that glowing renaissance of faith which had began some years before at Oxford, had fired Willie Felton strangely, and he thirsted to be among the heroes there himself. He and Lucy were never apart in the holiday time. They used to wander together for hours, exchanging their thoughts and aspirations, and Helen had never any share in these, either.

One drizzling afternoon, when the house was full of those popular but graceless acquaintances of Mr. Felton's, and the bitterness and family strife were drearier than ever, Lucy, walking the spongy red gravel paths through the garden, came upon Helen, shivering and lonely, seated on the mildewed benches of the temple of fraternal piety, which I suppose was empty of roots just then. The rattle of the distant shots came from over the misty covers on the hill top, and Helen, with her feet tucked under her and woe begone face, was listening to them for want of anything better to do. Little Lucy reflected that she was often sad herself, but the other seemed to be so much more forlorn. She went up to her according to her grave manner. " Can I help you, cousin ?" said she.

Helen looked up to discover if this were a taunt, then turned her head away, thinking to herself " If I had a papa and mamma to care for me, much I'd want your pity." " Oh !" she answered aloud, " I can keep my own sorrows, child," and gave the other a repelling look.

Lucy was very sorry ; but, because she was younger and by right looked down upon, had no appeal. Thus these two were never great friends. And Helen despised Cathy also, for, while she would often be dreaming all by herself, living for short moments in most perfectly happy places of her own making, the other would come begging her to listen to stories or answer silly questions ; George and Stephen had been meeter companions for her, since they, like her, used to be lonely and neglected.

Presently Mr. Felton sped away to Paris, and his wife once more appeared downstairs. A dreary noiseless party they made, the sallow little woman and the three old fashioned children, evening after evening, in the great half lit dining room. At intervals Lady Penelope would be heard scolding at the servants or complaining querulously of some troubles to poor Lucy, from whom she specially exacted sympathy. These were Helen's only companions day after day for the next two years. She had a share of the girls' governess and a share of their mother's temper, and all the time she was learning that quiet mental discipline which women have to be taught, though men may pick it up or not as chance guides them.

# CHAPTER V.

By and bye Lady Adelaide asked to have her little niece back at Sawtry again. She was very lonesome, she wrote. George was away with his uncle Ellis. They had taken him to Rome with them, first answering to his mother faithfully that he should be allowed to kiss no one's toe there. Stephen was still at Eton, and dearest Bertram, after a great many wild scrapes at Harrow, was to be an officer. He could hardly well stay on at school, and his father was sure they had treated him tyrannically. The Head Master had written—saying he would turn out either the best or the worst boy that ever was under him. They had tried for a commission in the Guards, but when Mr. Newmarch wrote to the Duke (who spent a day here years ago, when the two stags fought and were drowned in the lake) about it, they had got such a short answer. She wished she was like Mrs. Stacey, who could plague the Horse-Guards, and the Ministry, and the Admiralty, till she got everything for her sons. But as it was, Bertram had the choice of the Artillery, who were obliged to be so talented, or the Hussars, who were wicked.

It was a dilemma. However, with the hope that Bertram might perhaps show himself an exception to the rule amongst those godless horsemen, it was decided that he should have a cornet's commission. So Berty went down to Sandhurst one day with some blue documents in his pocket— shook hands with a pleasant gentleman standing before the fire—had some desultory conversation on arithmetic with a civil professor, and was told he had passed. Then came the pleasures of getting his smart uniform; and, though in those days tailors' bills were sometimes formidable, seldom had there been such a gallant figure fitted as his. When that was done his mother had a pretty waxy miniature done of him by Chalon at once. As he knew not how to hold himself like a soldier, it made him more like a chubby classic shepherd in gold lace, than anything else.

About the time Helen was to return, Berty

went off to join.    As  he drove away to Darying-worth,  the  world  was  for  him  the  brightest ever made.    A big cigar was in his mouth, plenty of money in his pocket, and the curling smoke of everybody's  admiration  about  him.    To  be  his own master, and growing  a  moustache,  only  a few months from the time  when  he had to rush down  to  the  Philathletic  field  after  four  Bill and crouch under a hedge with  a  row of shiver-ing companions, to smoke his pipe—while a felon bricklayer  was  hired  to  watch  from  the  nearest stile,  against  the  master's  approach—was indeed a  magical  transformation.    Of  course  he  gave Neal a parting sovereign.    His keeping accounts went  by  how  bulky  the  money  felt  inside  his pocket, and now  the  sovereigns  ground  against each  other  famously.    The  porters  all  knew Berty,  at  the  station,  and  lingered  with  curved palms,  at  the  carriage  door,  and  away  slid  the train—for  him  therefore,  bound  to  yonder  all glorious  untrodden  land,  where  one  is  for  ever young ;  where  no  accounts  have  to  be  rendered. He was now immortal so far,  with  the  power  of health  and  beauty  and  confidence.    Quite  sure, too,  that  everything  was  going  to  take  care  of itself and to come right.

When Helen appeared at Sawtry again, she had grown into a pretty pale young lady. It was quite correct to be interested in one so gentle and winning. The Squire took to noticing her specially, and it was his delight to call the attention of the company to her looks. "What causes them blushes on your cheeks now, Miss Helen?" he would say.

She, reproducing the phenomenon, would answer, "I don't know, uncle Brian."

"Don't know! Well you ought. I'm a going to ask the doctor to feel your pulse. What's the red dab that comes over your cheeks now?"

"I suppose it may be blood," she ventured, hoping to stop him.

"Well, to be sure! Why, blood comes from the heart, they tell me. What a soft heart this young lady must have, to be sure!"

However, these jokes, repeated thrice a day, would get a little wearisome. Sawtry was as lonely as ever, after Berty left. All the Feltons came by and bye, and Lady Penelope and her sister wrangled over their faiths and fancies when the squire was not present. After that Helen was again by herself as much as ever—for weeks and weeks there would be no change.  Willie Felton, she heard, had gone to Oxford, where he had joined the famous Regius Professor's disciples, and the accounts of his dress and doings used quite to take away Lady Penelope's breath.

George had come back from Italy with altered ideas, and after being a few weeks at Sawtry had gone into residence at Oxford, too.  He was a little lame still.  The thought of being a clergyman no longer chilled him as formerly; indeed, after he had been away with the Feltons certain things —the want of sympathy at home and his father's uncouth speeches—had given him many a pang. Neal said he could get no good out of Master George now, and thought of the old colt-breaking days with a sigh.  Yet he was just the same boy as when he went in the cheerless night to fetch his dear Berty a horse to hunt upon; only just now he was beginning to sift and riddle his brains to find a solution for all the questions opening before him—eager to hammer out a perfect system of morals from the rough blocks of ideas strewn thick before him.  At first, among those strange scenes—listening dreamily in the cold cathedral at Milan, his English hat uncomfortable in his hand, or hearing ghostly resurrection choruses in the Sixtine chapel—the sentimental glories of the novel Roman worship had taken a forcible grip on George's mind. Those attractive sights and sounds, the machinery of which is never explained—morticed into a long study of Newman, with his persuasive purity; Pugin, who with it all, he thought, never ceased to be an Englishman; Tennyson and Keble, Thomas Aquinas, Coleridge, and Carlyle—stirred his mind deeply. Oppressed by the aching horrors and meannesses that he saw with his fast opening eyes, he was sure that he could discover the remedy if only people would try, as he should, to do what was noble and pure. Strolling among the hawthorn trees at Sawtry he felt at this period like the discoverer of a new continent. He, for his part, longed to enlist under the banner of faith, to rush into the thick of the fight, wherever the foe was posted—sure now that he had solved most of the difficulties at last.

In this subjective paradise, fretting to be off, he had spent the time till Trinity term commenced, and then he was able to go up.

At Christ Church lots of old Eton friends were fallen upon again. Every one remembered Newmarch—who broke his leg playing at the wall—and it was pleasant to be a little distinguished hobbling down the High. George, in those days, was as exclusive in his choice of a friend as of a tailor. Anything scoffing or unearnest was repellant to him. I think when he read Samuel Warren just then, he was as good a Tory as Lord Eldon; and by and bye " Alton Locke " made him a scoffing socialist in its turn.

Those were very happy days, and none the less that, while occupied with crusades, debts will begin to gather in swarms. But George could never bear anything very common or tawdry about him, and, although bread and cheese for himself would have made him quite happy when no one was by—yet when his friends met at his board they should see that he, indeed, had ' learnt to dine.' It happened that more than once a departing scout robbed poor George, and many of his prettiest medieval chattels had to be renewed. By and bye people said that Newmarch chucked his money about—for a younger son—and laughed at him freely. Yet in one's first term at Oxford, creditors are in the conditional mood, most inoffensive; and George arranged with himself that, by and bye, when he had got everything he wanted, he would lie to and pay off those stupid bills by degrees. Being thus prosperous he could afford to be generous as well.

Now there had been at George's tutor's at Eton a puny, forsaken little boy, whom he had hardly known. Remembered merely as being shabby and oppressed, he now turned up at Christ Church a dandy of the first water. After a while even, by virtue of having grown on to have a smart figure, planting out the worst part of his face with curly, golden whiskers, and being besides the nephew and heir to a peer, he had made a certain way for himself and come to patronise his old acquaintances. The boy, too, had an air of having his eyes wider open, and of knowing the world better than other men of his college; there was a calm indifference to business, to worry, or to misfortune about him, which, in his friends' eyes, partook somewhat of the sublime.

"What a dirty little cad, one remembers Algy Woodville at school," says the Honourable Jack Talfrey, filling his pipe as he stood at George's window one morning, after a breakfast in the latter's rooms.

Said young Watkin Watkin, who had a large comprehensive faith in these mysterious beings who really saw life and knew everybody, "Don't know what you call a cad, Jack, but there ain't many things Algy ain't fly to, I know."

George's window happened to be in a re-entering corner of the quadrangle, and, on a level with them, they could just see into Mr. Woodville's room, where that young gentleman, in a violet satin morning jacket, was having an interview with Bob Tramp, the horse dealer. "Look at him!" went on Jack. "How that other fellow keeps bowing and bobbin' his head. Wish he'd stop."

"Daresay there's some of Algy's 'good things' being planned," said Watkin Watkin, in a tone of awe. "He's sure to keep it to himself though, that's the worst of him—" All this did not please George very much; he returned to the table and resumed his beer and the poet whose leaves he was cutting.—"Ever hear of Algy going to Baden," continued Watkin Watkin, mysteriously. "Fellow in the 10th told me about it, was there at the time. First day he began, he won two thousand straight off. Left half of it with his banker in the town and kept the rest to go on with. In twenty-four hours loses that,—draws out t'other,—loses that too, and every penny he had at home besides."

" What did he do next?" ₁asks Jack, rather impressed.

" Why, he finished the winter at Melton with a dozen hunters. And 'twould take a deuced hard man to beat him, when the hounds were really running, I've heard. Knows everything I do believe, Jack. You ask him the rights of this last story about Lady Mary Tarlatan jilting young Fitzbud; or who gives Zoë Davis all her diamonds. Or who's going to win the Derby—I do believe he knows that too."

" Ah! I daresay," said Jack, shaking his head. and thinking of the mutations in human fortune after Algy's Eton reputation.

But these, George said, were dull and revolting topics to him. The boy's utter confidence and indifference was a sort of study, however. George pitied him and would now and then give him a word of advice ; and their rooms being near each other, he would sometimes take in a book at night, and, if he found Algy alone, would endeavour to share his interest in anything that struck him as beautiful with his young friend.

Being in London for a day or two once, George went with his Aunt Ellis in Napthali's great shop. Three fine young gentlemen behind the counter attended to Lady Blanche's endless directions about the mending of a twopenny brooch which she especially wished justice done to, and George stood, rather awed by the blaze of gilding, marble, and glass in the place. Looking round suddenly, he saw Algy Woodville, and a tall young man—sprawling over a lot of jewellery and indeed occupying a whole counter themselves. "Halloa, Newmarch!" says Algy, turning from the heaps of enchanting things laid out upon the white wadding before him. "You go in for some of these—buy the whole population of Woodstock straight off. I say, come and dine with me to-night."

"Thank you," said George, not very enthusiastically.

"At seven, mind—at Buffer's. Because I've got a box for the play. Look here, I haven't ordered very much. Anything you like to drink, you know. I forget if you know Newmarch, Teddington?"

The other nodded to George and turned to the radiant *employé*, saying "I want my bill, by the way, you sent me one a year ago?"

"Oh! those fellows up there, I suppose," the

gentleman of the place answered, nodding contemptuously towards a gallery, where a row of clerks were busily writing, "they will amuse themselves making those things out, but no one takes the slightest notice of them."

"All right, send it, though," said the Marquis.

"Who was your friend, George?" asked his aunt when they were in the carriage.

"Oh! Algy Woodville, a man at my college."

"The other was Lord Teddington, was it not? No friend for you, I fear."

"Well, I don't know," said George; "he gave a blank cheque to build a church at Shaffham, you remember;" but Lady Blanche shook her head.

Mr. Ellis, for George's benefit, suggested something to the butler about a latch key. But the idea was received with pain. Such a thing had not been heard of there for years. The notion was monstrous. That great black door, between those sentinel extinguishers, being asked to open on a novel principle, at the small hours, to a flighty undergraduate! Fortunately, Algy Woodville got helpless very early at dinner and fancied he was going to get one of his attacks of the heart, so George having seen him to bed was glad to escape early. Next day he called to see how he was, about eleven o'clock. There he lay, in bed, as cheery as ever. "Dine with me, to-night," said he. "You don't mind, eh? Look, I can't dine alone these times."

Then they had a chat and Algy dressed.

"Oh! by the way," said he, as they were just leaving the room, "you mind doing something for me? you mind backing a bill for me? I must pay three hundred into Reed's bank to-day, or I'm done for. There's a fellow coming about the bill—expect him every minute."

George opened his eyes. Back a bill! This was something he had read of—but never come across in real life as yet. But then a generous feeling crept over him.

"I suppose I won't have to pay, eh?" said he.

"No, not you," says Woodville. "I shall take it up—before it is due, I think."

Then he gave a graphic sketch of the hopeless plight he just happened to be in at that moment. This was the sort of man for whom George sacrificed himself. Within an hour he had signed his name across a promissory note drawn by

Algy Woodville, thus :—" Accepted.—Payable at Wynn Ellis and Co. "GEO. C. NEWMARCH."

"You had better say Wynn Ellis," remarked Algy, "because they're relations, you know."

There was another paper to sign—a declaration from George that he was of age. "But it was a lie," he had said.

Whereupon Algy had whistled and shrugged his shoulders. "Well, old boy, it's clean ruin to me, you know," he said, quietly. And George pitied him from the bottom of his soul.

'It was a mere matter of form,' explained the bill stealer and tout whom they were with.

George therefore signed his first lie.

Their dinner at Buffer's was very gloomy that evening. This lie kept glistening on the table cloth before him. "And," said he to himself, "I suppose Woodville thinks it's my paltry money I'm anxious, and wretched, and guilty about!" He wished he had never partaken of the slang splendours of Buffer's— ere half the dinner was out, though there was a marquis at the next table and some young men from Windsor were also present, full of the best information on some races which were shortly to be held there.

Somehow, at Christ Church, he felt a repugnance for Algy after that.   The latter would now do anything for George—in reason, and vowed that he was really a much better fellow than people imagined.   But George felt shy in Algy's presence and afraid of him, henceforward.   The time to meet the bill flew.   Before George had thought much of it, it was long vacation.

Just before leaving for home George wrote for permission to bring a man from college with him. Not a Christ Church man, he said, but his especial friend, Cyril Wilson.   It had been George's great delight to tell this companion of his walks all about Sawtry, about the things to be seen there, jollier than anywhere else—and which he looked forward to showing to him, when they had time to themselves.

Lovely the place did look in the sun, the June afternoon that they arrived.   There was a grave, ancient air of rest all about the house; then it was " Home,"—which is indeed the ' argument' of a long Poem.   They found the squire in the library, where a fire was still kept up—groaning and muttering to himself, for he was just then reading over some of his eldest son Berty's letters about money.   " Well, made a Papist of you, have they?" said he, peering up at George.

"How you've grown. Seen your mother yet? She'll be raising the house, I suppose, when she hears you've come. Why, here's another fine young man," he continued, when George said,—"This is Mr. Wilson, papa." George's friend had a cheery, confident way of looking at things, and was proud of his calling as an undergraduate. But these were subjective gifts. "Well, sir, how do you do? I'm glad to see you. Are you a Papist, too?" was the squire's greeting to him.

"'Pon my word, sir, rather a leading question, that," answered the young man, saying to himself that this was a Tory of the port drinking school. "The Roman schism is a great fact, I think, sir, in these days, and 'pon my word, we at Oxford have begun to say that 'Catholic' includes what is best in both of us you know, sir. I'm afraid George here 'll agree with me, that it wouldn't be the fashion for us, to be burnt 'over against Baliol College,' as hot gospellers, now-a-days."

"They don't want to burn you," said the squire, who was thinking of his letters. "They'd ha' put you young gentlemen in the village pound with nothin' but thistles, I'm thinking; but how do I know what you may be going to be?" he muttered.

This was rather discouraging. To be sure, how could the old man appreciate a development far withdrawn from his own narrow grove of thought.

" I hope we'll make better acquaintance with each other's views then, sir," the younger man suggested, as cheerfully as he could.

" Well, you may try," muttered the squire, getting up.  " I'm getting old to begin."

Then he walked away growling.  This failure made George very unhappy; it was a blow to him, counting, as he did, on presenting every-thing to his friend in a pleasant light.

" Come and see the horses, Cyril, old boy," said he, as cheerfully as he could, and they went across the garden.

Cyril thought such a lovely spot was worth coming any distance to see.

" Aye, isn't it a jolly place to lie with a book, old boy?" George answered.

The fountain near them pattered in one's ears, gossipping to the sun; and if you lay on the grass with your eyes turned up, birds and bees came and went, staring at you.

While they stood open eyed, Miss Helen came through the door, pinning her dress against a nail as she passed. It was a Holland frock, on which the shadows of the leaves made cool splashes, while her hat and hair were in the sun. She was looking down. She had grown so fine a young lady that George said to himself he did not know her. The two friends stood and observed her. Poor Cyril Wilson fell in love with her. George gazed, but he was thinking of the whole place, of his home and the beauty of it.

Then he went forward and had twenty questions to ask her, and she told him all the Sawtry news, laughing and blushing at every second word. But "there is a gulf between us," thought George. As for Cyril—as remarked above—he was greatly in love with Helen by dressing time, and with a towel, and a razor, and one boot in his hand, formulated a romance in which he and she were the only two characters.

As for Helen, Bully, a fine bull dog, had been her only companion lately. Now George was come, he should go about with her. The summer is the pleasantest time for girls, one can sit under the trees working or reading, or can walk in dry places. Now, in winter, one must sit and shiver over the fire unless one affects to like riding over great hedges hunting.   George and Helen moved about unnoticed.   Sometimes the squire would order the horses for them; other days would vow that they should walk, as far as he was concerned, for the rest of their lives.   Cyril Wilson remained but a few days, and never tried to banter his host again.   During his stay he went through all the stages of a great passion, whereof the brown e yed Helen was the object, and at the time of driving away to the station at Daryngworth, had just reached the stage of courageous, hopeless resignation. ' Of course,' he said, ' it was not meet that it should be,' and in the railway carriage—on the back of an envelope rested on the crown of his hat, strove to plait the threads of his despair into a string of verses.   " A strong heart in dry places,"  the lines were to be called, but in those days, Great Northern carriages rattled so, that the lines were never completed.

# CHAPTER VI.

IF George could have forgotten that bill, he would have been very happy then. Of course, before a week he had made Helen his confidant. Riding through Chartloe Park, one day, he told her all about it. The worst was that he could not get her to comprehend the rights of it, and she was only terrified. But for the lie, it would have been nothing. All his friends would have that in their thoughts when they came to meet him by and bye. And it was a lie. What would he not give to be really twenty-one. Why didn't the law make people of nineteen of age, he would complain to Helen, and then would stay silent for a long time, whereupon she had to keep silent too.

No one except the squire noticed much that they rode together in the warm evenings till

lights were out in the sitting rooms.    It seemed
to amuse him.

" Oh ! Lord," he used to say, when Helen came
down to breakfast.  " She blushes  these times,
worse than ever."

George fell in love with Helen.    But it took
Lady Adelaide a long time to know that.    Why,
they all saw the girl every day, and  who should
ever think of being in love with her ?   Again, she
herself had not been  brought into  contact with
love matters for some thirty-eight years.    Helen
and George were children still in her eyes.    Who
could feel anxious about them ?

" You'll be havin' a match  to talk over soon,
milady," observed the  squire, walking into his
wife's  boudoir  one  day  from  quarter  sessions.

She could not think which one he meant.

" Well, perhaps not.  I'll be writin' to my lord
Newbury, to ask what he'll give the girl  if she'll
have my son George,'' he went on.  " He  hasn't
heard her name once since she came to this house
first, but maybe he's thinking all the more—who
knows ?  Henry Stacey told me on  the bench
to-day that Sims, Long, and Walter had orders to
refuse an offer of a  hundred thousand pounds for

that Wallsacre property of your brother's. If he
had let States have it, there'd have been some
decent cottages built, perhaps."

"You take my senses away, Brian," said his
wife. "Pray reflect before you talk of such
madness as writing to Edmund on such a
subject. Was there anything special at quarter
sessions ?"

"Not a thing. Lord Knaresborough has
twelve men in Daryngworth gaol for poaching. I'll
be a chartist soon, milady."

But Lady Adelaide was thinking of other
things.

"I wonder where those two are now." she
mused, a little startled, though she would not
allow it, by her husband's words. Meantime,
this beautiful summer's day, Helen and George
walked down to the boat house, away from everybody else, as happy as the rabbits or the birds.

Charming was the grass they walked upon ;
charming were the trees ; and they, no doubt,
perfect. It was delightful, shooting out of the
dark boat shed, on to the broad lake ; and a
smile of sheer happiness came budding on the
face of each. Helen could not trim the boat to
George's critical taste exactly. He felt as if he

could scull for a week, he said, and didn't feel the heat one bit.   She amused him.

The sun fell on her face, and looking at her with the easy insolence of health, he began,

"How you blink your big eyes, Helen!"   She put up a shabby little parasol; whereon said he, "When you come to Oxford, I'll get you another of those!"

"Oh! you won't, I think."

"Why?"

"Because Lucy and Catherine Felton are coming to commemoration too, and you'll be afraid."

"Afraid!"

"Look," said Helen, "this is where I used to come with Willie and Edith Basledon, when you were abroad.   My! my! how they used to go on—and then have such fights!   This was their boat, too; what trouble I got into about them," and she smiled pensively.

George didn't care to hear about them.

"Don't you like sticking your arms into the cool water, Helen.   Look here—you do it now."

"No, I won't!"

"Why, you've got muscles on your arm like the Tipton Slasher.   Ever hear of him?"

"Let my arm alone, George.   You'll upset the boat and ruin one's dress besides."

It was not impossible; the more so as he could not keep steady and touch her arm too. "How she opens her brown eyes," he thought, "she has no eyebrows either!"

Before them, the head of the lake was in a white haze under the sun.   At that farthest end, where they now were, is a little island grown with dark green trees; its shelving banks are red, and the water is glassy green up to where you land.

"Let us stop and live here," said George. "I daresay it won't be so hot.   Oh, my! how close it is, Helen!"

"Willie took me here once," said she.

"Did he confou—" She laughed.  George was not jealous, however—not he.   He knew women too thoroughly, for had he not been some considerable time at college?   And look what all the books say about them.   Their schemes are shewn up in many books.—"And here's where Willie and I found an echo—"

The place was quite still ; not a sound, save a leaf falling into the water or a bee flying about. Helen had her work, and George strolled about in his shirt sleeves. "What an innocent child," mused he, "and what a shame it would be of anyone to make love to the little friendless girl merely for fun. How jolly she does look, though. What a hot oppressive day it is, and—what does it matter after all?" So he went and sat on the grass near her.—"I say, you've got on a pretty gown for once !'

" 'Tisn't a gown, it's a dress."

" Well, a dress. I'll get a jacket made of that stuff, when I go back—for the river."

Then he took away her little hat and gave her his, with a Ch. Ch. ribbon round it.—"I say, Helen, what funny gloves."—Shabby brown thread gloves those. Yet they contained enough to make his hand tremble, when he touched them ; and his voice would falter.

"You needn't break my fingers !"

" Why, you said as much as *that* couldn't hurt you. Tell me—why doesn't Lady Adelaide give you parasols and everything ?"—

" She's very good to me."

" Not quarter good enough. Why did she send away the maid you used to have after you came from Rushworth? I heard of that. I pity that maid."—Her buff coloured hair, he thought, he might just touch. From it little sprays fell on to her forehead, and George smoothed them away with his finger tips.—" Fancy, never brushing this hair any more!" he said, with a husky voice. ' It's very jolly this, but I wish I wasn't afraid of her,' said he, within his heart of hearts.

" Fancy, to be sure! The idea's terrible," Helen answered—saying to herself, ' He's laughing at me, I am sure.'—" Give me back my hat, George, and don't hurt my fingers. You make the rings dig into my flesh." And she put on such a face, and showed him little pink scars upon her fingers; then laid her head upon the grass and shut her eyes.

All the lake spread out under them, hazy with a summer heat, and Helen lay with a flush of sunburn on her forehead. Gentle forehead! When he touched it lightly he had felt his hand tingle. The little person shut her eyes while he thus looked upon her; then, biting a laugh, pretended to breathe as though fast asleep; whereupon came a coiling serpent, some yards long, and said to George,—" Look, undergraduate; kiss her pretty cheek while she lies warm and pink asleep." But this timid one trembled in the grasp of temptation. He dared not stoop and touch her guileless face. Perhaps she might rise indignant, like a person in a Play. So, gazing on her rather sheepishly, he drew away, consoled to think that it was his mighty self denial kept his lips away. "I was a fraid," he should have said. And she, motionless, with her head among the little flowers, and close shut eyes, wondering what might be passing above, breathed softly, till at last her eyes. opening, she saw him more ill at ease than usual, his head turned towards the lake, and chucking pebbles into the water. Then she, being 'eternally unkissed,' they began talking together once more. And a faint conversation it was, he wondering, in a choking sort of voice—if it were late. Next minute she remarked, "Perhaps it is getting late," and after a while he said, "It must be rather late;" and each speech of his should have been, "What a perfect little darling you are, Helen."

But they were not capable of interpreting these speeches, and the day being nearly gone, silent, he rowed her home. 'She surely,' said he, 'ought to understand.' As they landed at last, perhaps he was not sorry to be clear of his perplexities and her fascinations. He formulated for his vanity's sake, that—'Women are a bore,'—but—'I might

have had one little kiss,'—he added, to his very
inmost self. We never know what she thought,
poor child!

When the young people got upstairs there was
not much doubt that it was late. George's heart
beat—he did not exactly know why—and as they
stood at the dining-room door, irresolute—out
came a footman bearing a huge tray, escorted by
the butler—swearing at the man in the softest
tone for letting the glasses rattle. "Oh! it's
Master George. Very late, sir," he said, with a
respectful grin, and held the door open for them.

In walked the guilty pair, bringing a dead
silence with them, Lady Adelaide, the Squire, Mr.
Curry, the Rector, and Colonel Pagnel—who had
come over from Chartloe to fish—all looking up
at them.

"Hum!" says the squire, "Simmonds."

"Yes, sir."

"Give 'em their dinner on the sideboard."

His wife gave him a look. George shook hands
with each of the guests, saying hardly a word;
and poor Helen went up to Lady Adelaide to
whisper a sort of apology. "Yes, of course,
dear," said the lady, and turned to Mr. Curry
with a word or two to break the silence. After

which she rose and was going, taking Helen with her.

" Well, Miss Helen, did you find any mistletoe, now?" says the Squire, as she passed his chair.

Poor Helen looked for some chance of escape. But finding none, halted under the Squire's glances—turning pale as a sheet.

" Come here," said he, " I'll tell you about Julia Tresham, that fat old maid,—well, you don't know her—and she was walking with Charles Paston in my park here—and so she went close up to an oak tree. ' Dear me, what's that growing on the tree, Sir Charles?' she says. An' so he looked an' looked, like a booby. ' I can't see,' he says, ' shall I ask the gardener, Miss Tresham?' and he puts up his glasses. ' Oh! you silly man,' she said—' why, it's mistletoe!' Wasn't he silly?"

" What an ancient scandal, Squire," said the Colonel; and at last Helen was released.

What passed between the two ladies is not disclosed; at all events, poor Helen was not supposed to want any dinner at all that day, while George, on the contrary, with a fair appetite, induced Simmons to bring him some soup, a couple of cutlets, and a portion of currant tart, which he consumed, thinking much of elective affinities the while.

Next day Lady Adelaide was far from well, and Helen, of course, could not leave her much through the forenoon. Nothing touched the Squire's cynical humour better than to watch Helen and George, not saying a word to each other when they met.

" I never could have suspected one of my sons of such conduct," was all Lady Adelaide said publicly at this time, and George found nothing to answer to her; but it may be that all this fixed the sunny afternoon on the island all the firmer in his imagination.

Of course his mother behaved like a sensible person, and some three or four days later called George into her room, and gave him a letter from Aunt Ellis, begging as a special favour that he might be allowed to come to her in London before the season was quite over. Christ Church men were always in such request; and then her little people had quite gone into raptures when they heard that Cousin George was coming again.

Meanwhile, while Mr. Algernon Woodville and his companions were living on rye bread, cream, yördbeerea, and Fortnum and Mason's stores in a

Norwegian shanty—killing fish, learning ballads, and smoking wooden pipes—the dingy gang who went about with George's acceptance in their dirty pocket books, had duly presented that paper at Wynn Ellis's, where poor George, knowing no other Banker, had been advised by Algy to make it payable. " It was a most pain-ful affair," Mr. Ellis had remarked, but business was business—the bill must either be refused or paid over the counter, and so the holder received it back into his hands with an ugly postcript pinned on to it, " No orders; refer to drawer." Mr. Ellis could only take some steps to find out who it was held the bill, and then write at once to Sawtry.

The inevitable Post is sure to bring its mes-sage of trouble or of pleasure in due course, and there lay the Banker's letter next morning by the Squire's plate, side by side with a couple of begging letters, a prospectus of a Freehold Chapel to be sold, and a rudely worded bill "for cropping two teryer pups eers, and their tails bit."

The Squire, it happened, shuffled in very late, and George, having no appetite to delay him, strolled off towards the boat-house, thinking he'd just scull up to that island once again.

Then the squire opened his letters, and neither swore nor said very much.

"This is a desperate blackguard business," he muttered several times, and fancied the very worst of his son as he sat in the library thinking it over. But George was lying the while on the island, close by the very spot, trying to bring that happy afternoon all back again. "Here she rested her little head," he mused—and sighed and sighed, as the fashion has always been. Then, returning sheepishly towards the house, he was met by a bare headed footman, and summoned before his father. As he pushed open the door,—"What a waste life would be without her," he thought.

"Read that," said the Squire, with a look not often on his face. "You're beginning early, sir, to be a swindler and a blackguard."

"Eh?" says George, with eyes staring, and indeed struck rigid, as he held the letter open in his hand. "A swindler?" he asked, as if the word held him down to the ground. He feared his father much, but these horrible names seemed superior to his awe. "I'm not a swindler," he began, rapidly. "Who says it? I only helped him," and then he caught hold of the table, breathing so fast that he could not go on talking.

" Well, sir," thundered the Squire, "what do I want of your airs! You go and draw on a Bank where you've got no funds, and may—d'you hear?—be had up for felony ; aye, and worse, no doubt, behind this, that I don't know of. Now, sir, who's Mr. Woodville, and who's all your infernal friends together?"—George could not answer. Had he done all this? It might be. He had known he must suffer—ever since that day with Algy, and he supposed he deserved it all. " I'll tell you, sir," he said, chokingly, "if you won't call me a swindler." And then he gave a hurried, vague account of the bill story, forgetting half of it in his eagerness.

" I believe you are telling me a lie—aye, a dozen," said his father ; and George shivered down to the soles of his feet.

" I shall write to this Woodville's father, and to Lord Mountjoy. You'll be very welcome at your Aunt Blanche's, I'm thinking. It's a proud thing for me to have my family name hawked about among all the thieves in London. That'll do—I don't want you ; you are a bit of a liar, I think."

So the horrid scene had ended, and George went out, believing himself to be a thief. There was one consolation, though, for him : he would never see his uncle Ellis again—never bring disgrace on them by entering their doors. No, he had done with it all. He left the house, and strode on up the park—behind the house, through the long grass—till the beating of his heart forbid his going on. Then, with breakers of fierce thought quarrelling in his brain, he turned and looked back. Was it for this reward he had done his best and kept his ways? Had his self-examinations and his denials of many things come to this—" a swindler and a blackguard?" He remembered all the " blackguards" he had known of. They told him he was one of these. They were the ones who consorted together in greasy billiard rooms, and smoked, and cursed—and sneered with familiar glee, over bills, and duns, and horrors of every kind, having no friends save but appalling horse jockeys and barmaids.

Resting there by a thorn tree, he looked below and saw where the white stone house stood out above the garden tree tops, against the dark back ground of wood and meadow, and he almost cursed it all; then leant his forehead on his burning hands. " God forgive me, I would be patient if I could; and I will still," he said.

It was his first bitter revolt against the old tyranny of reaping as one sows. And now blaming most of all the cruel way his crop had grown and ripened, he rose, and slowly went back down the hill, climbed the sunk fence, and got into the garden out of sight of the house.

By and bye, pacing the walk with his head down, George came upon his mother, and would have liked to pass her without a word. " My darling," she said, and took his hot, brown hands in hers, and kissed them. Strange! so there was some one who did love him after all ?— but when his mother began to speak kindly of his going to London, avoiding the topic that they both were thinking of, " Nothing in the world," he said, " would induce him to go to his aunt's now. He would do anything rather ; Australia was not so very far."

" Very well, my boy; stay with me, then," she said, and kissed him again.

They were a silent party at dinner that day and the next. The third day George was staring out of the window after breakfast, cooling his forehead against the glass; he was thinking how his father had not spoken to him once since the day that letter had come, and his mother only a word of pity occasionally. " I wish to God I were dead," he moaned.

" George !" he heard a wee voice say ; and when

he looked round, there stood the little Helen, all by herself, dressed to go out, and looking very grave; perhaps somewhat frightened to be alone with George, now.

"Where are you off to, cousin?" he asked, in wonder.

"I'm going to Aunt Penelope's to-day," she answered. "I think it is time to start now."

He turned away from her, and leaned his forehead on his arms. Of course that came on him, too, because he liked her.

"We should say good-bye, George," said Helen meekly, interrupting his reflections.

He turned once more, and stared at her, a most troubled look upon his face.

"Good-bye."

"Good-bye."

They shook hands; but when he felt hers, hot and trembling --"Nothing more," he said, with the inspiration of despair, and drew her towards him.

But the traditional awe of these processes had descended to Helen; she turned very pale. "Oh! let me go," she said, and dragged her hand away. Yet stayed one minute longer; and he looked so profoundly sad.

"Oh! my heart is breaking!" she heard him mutter. This is known to be figurative; but she thought it might break—and so kill him, poor old fellow. Was he not to be deeply pitied, then? "If you will not keep me long, you may," she faintly whispered, to her own immense surprise. George turned, hardly able to see her, and while she hung down her head, gave her an eager kiss, which begun at the corner of her eyebrow —slipped down on to her cold cheek. With his brain throbbing, and his eyes burning hot, he waited there until he heard the carriage wheels grind on the gravel before the house. 'Over his heart they rolled,' he thought; and she was gone.

And now, as the unfeeling days came and went, he began to settle that life was a Blank to him, indeed. His heart strings were torn, he said—or rent, that was a better word. He would never marry now—never; and it was as well, since the church was to be his bride. He came to think it would not be so hard to walk with those who had adopted the Roman Obedience—in the matter of Priestly celibacy, at any rate; and that sweet tenet was often borne on his heart now. He resolved that he would open his conscience to Mr.

Curry about this, for he felt more and more daily the need of that direction which his Priest could, of his office, best give him.

One day, therefore, he strolled down the avenue, and a little way up the pretty dusty village road to the rectory. This was to be George's home some day. It always was a quiet spot. Ah! how meek and lovely Helen would have looked, standing before the laurels to welcome him there some day. But since it was not well that it should be so, what were all the bright lawn and metal-green walls of holly to him?

Mr. Curry, as has been said, held the living of Sawtry Marshal under a bond of resignation, till George was fit to be presented to it. He was a widower, with nine grown-up children—perhaps, in some respects, just the counsellor George needed. The single-hearted man was in his garden, with his coat off, watering a bed of tulips—a well-thumbed book in his other hand. "Eh! that you, George—you never come to pay me a visit now," said he, peering up from behind his spectacles. "Here's some tulips your mamma gave me, boy; aren't they getting on? Never tired of Jeremy Taylor, are you? Out of date, though, with you modern young fellows at Oxford, I'm afraid."

And he went on chatting simply till George led the conversation very diplomatically up to the subject with which his mind was occupied.

"Eh! my opinion?" says Mr. Curry, starting at one of George's questions. Then he gave a sigh. "Well, about marriage; it's a serious thing." He mused for a while, and added innocently, "Well, boy, if you ask me—what with journeys to the sea side, and the doctor's bill, and that grasping female—the monthly nurse, I mean, boy, she was an intemperate woman—from Fettergay—Ah! you didn't know her.—Yes, each of these emergencies must have cost forty pounds, George. And then there was poor dear Eliza's eldest sister Of course I couldn't refuse to have her here—always glad to see her for poor Eliza's sake—and what with her flys from the station, and flys back, and the flymen's beer— Ah! my boy, I don't know—don't you think you ought to consider a while, eh?"

George gave a pitying smile of acquiescence.

"Yes," Mr. Curry added, scratching the back of his neck thoughtfully, with a corner of Jeremy Taylor; "poor dear Eliza's sister was a trial in many ways. I can't say I asked her; and yet she ended her days in that front room where you see the window open, George. Four different complaints, boy, and the doctor's bill. Ah! me—yes; she bore it with a little show of temper at times. But 'twas all before your day, boy."

It was a disappointment, and a hard one, to George, and as soon as he could leave without offending the rector, he went ruefully back again. And this, then, was the mundane view people took of those things! George betook himself to the shadiest part of the garden to ponder over a volume of "Plain Sermons," and another of Peter Dens, with "Lewis Aloysius Newmarch," in faded writing on the fly leaf.

Meanwhile, the squire had received Lord Mountjoy's frank reply to the letter which he had written about Algy Woodville's bill—dated from his lordship's villa at Sorrento.

" Sir,—

" I have no knowledge whatever of the young gentleman referred to in your letter, except that he is son to my brother, Mr. Henry Woodville.

" I am, your obedient servant,

" Mountjoy."

" Brian Newmarch, Esq."

And from Henry Woodville, the father —nothing at all.   The son, apparently, was altogether unattainable.

After that, Mr. Newmarch was obliged, reviling those gentlemen the while, to leave the matter in his own lawyer's hands, and then fresh miserable scenes ensued at Sawtry.

The affair, to be sure, was simple enough. George, clearly not being of age, and having signed a document to the effect that he *was*, had rendered himself liable to the criminal charge of obtaining money under false pretences.   The bill people could wait, as they had got hold of a good man now; meanwhile, there was endless interest running on.   There wasn't the smallest chance of resisting the claim.   They were the very worst gang of bill-stealers in London, the lawyers wrote, and apparently prepared to swear that George had received the whole of the money consideration for the bill himself.   About that time, I think, Algy Woodville killed a forty-six pound fish on the Great Tana river in Finmark.   He was not coming back to Oxford, but he wrote an account of his exploits to one or two fellows there, having actually, he said, to send his letter by a chance Whaler from that remote stream.

It was a toss up at one time whether the squire washed his hands of the whole thing, and allowed a warrant to be taken out against his son. If any-one had given him advice, or pleaded the boy's cause, he probably would. One day, however, in a more savage humour than usual, he sent for George. "Here," said he; "I'm just going to send off a cheque for this three hundred and ninety-seven pounds to my precious lawyers. I suppose you'd soon earn that sum at Christ Church now."

"I cannot earn money there," said George; "but I can go to Australia, and—"

"Well, I don't think you can. You'll just go where I tell you. Well, you may mean well, for all I know, and now your name comes off the books at Christ Church at once, and you'll finish your learning at St. Abb's College. It's a very fine place, I'm told, and when this money's stopped out of your allowance, you'll start fair again. That's what you'll do."

Then, with a few more directions and remarks of the same kind, George's fate was decided, and he was to see Oxford no more.

What could he answer to all this? He was too proud to take his punishment crying out. This was it—nothing romantic or quickly over

even; no banishment to toil and adventure at
sea, or in new lands: a fate like that would
have had a kind of charm for George.  But to go
and live—as he put it at once—among cads, in
that awful place which he had just heard talked
of, no one that he could even speak to—and all
this instead of the charming days at Christ
Church with gentlemen and people that could appreciate him and whom he could admire.  And
then, to have no money at all.  How were even
his Oxford debts to be confessed?  No; he would
never endure the slow degradation and shabby
misery of it all—never.  He moodily sought out
the map of the world, and travelled away South
with his finger—till he landed in Melbourne, and
was away, in imagination, from debts, and swind-
ling friends, and people judging him harshly,—
cracking his stock whip—wandering over endless
prairies where a scythe had never been, after
flocks of sheep who would arise without tiresome
capital—doing anything, in fact.  And yet how
wretched it all was, and quite barren he felt were
the uses of adversity to him.  He was only
angry, and when he was trying to read and store
his mind with better things, or would gladly have
been dwelling on the image of Helen sitting on

the island in her one sole  pretty dress, his own misfortunes and petty cares forced it all from him.   He had signed his name to a lie that could not be got over ; but still  it was  because he was generous, and tried to  help a friend, that trouble came on him.   For days together he would be racking his brains in that fashion without time to think of his Love.   But her memory, he used to say, would never, never fade.

## CHAPTER VII.

WHEN the wagonette, bringing Miss Mallorie from the Railway Station, came into Rushworth Park, Lady Penelope saw it—a speck on the white carriage drive. " Who can this be?" she said, fidgeting. " Dear, dear, me! more visitors; and, why !—in our carriage, too. Can it be one of my daughters, Julia ?"

" But, Lady Penelope," Miss Tresham answered, " Lucy and Catherine were here not a moment since."

" Ah! yes—it's very provoking of people."

The two ladies were sitting in the shade of the house before the open drawing-room windows, Miss Tresham committed for the afternoon to some book which Willie Felton had advised her to read. It was so hot one could not walk. By and bye the wagonette came to the bridge, and pulled up to cross it slowly.

"I said it was that child, Helen Mallorie. To be sure it is," said Lady Penelope, as though she had talked of nothing else for an hour. "I remember now; some crotchet of Adelaide's sending the girl. Her sulky son George formed an attachment. Nothing was to be said about it, please Julia. She should have grown up very pretty; can you tell me?"

How could she possibly know, Miss Tresham reflected; but it was useless entering into things with Penelope. "Was her mother a Lisle?" she asked.

"Eh? was she? Anne Newbury's sister. I never approved of Edmund's choice. We dined thirteen at table the day he and the bride came back from Venice."

And then it struck Miss Tresham that she had been in the house for a week, and no one had seemed to expect Miss Mallorie at all. She supposed the girl was a little neglected. "Does your brother take much interest in his niece?" she asked.

Lady Penelope may have recognised a gentle curiosity here to learn whether the young lady was likely to be an heiress; but she was not in the same polite humour.—"Forgets her name," she said, bluntly. "We used to think he had affection,—for the mother's sake, but that seems over long ago. Adelaide has brought the child up. The fact is, no one knows quite what Edmund's life is, or what connections he may have formed. There'll be immense accumulations of personalty—eh, isn't it?—but the title goes to Blanche and her son, of course."

Then the carriage passed close, and Miss Tresham noticed a pretty face smiling towards Lady Penelope. "Dear, dear! did they send you all the way by yourself?" said the flighty little woman, kissing Miss Helen. "You must be as tall as Lucy;—is Brian getting old?—has Mrs. Stacey many eldest sons staying at Bullingworth? Ah! I forgot—it's the London season, child. You won't mind having the blue dressing-room? Miller! Miller! where are the young ladies?"

This was a great amount of cordiality for Lady Penelope; and Helen was grateful. Of course, she must put up with knocking about from one house to another, since it appeared that Lord Newbury had quite forgotten her. Her aunt looked altered and old. "How I remember that gown she has on," thought Helen. "It had crape when Maud Ellis died; before it used to be trimmed with ruches of green satin. She had it turned the second winter I was here; the skirt was a dinner dress once, wasn't it?—yes."—

But at that moment came her two cousins welcoming her.

Cathy couldn't say how delighted she was, and kissed and kissed. "My pretty dear!" said Lucy in her inimitable voice, "we never hoped we were to have you so soon—did we, Cathy? You owe me three letters, do you know, Miss Helen."

They were glad enough of another companion, at weariful Rushworth. I think Helen must have acquired grown up arts by this, for, though she did not care a button for the voice or its owner, she was all smiles and affection in her turn.

"So Mr. Felton's away," she concluded, inwardly. "There'll be none of that weary duty in the store-room then. Cathy 'll never be the least pretty I see. Lucy is quite lovely—if only her eyes were darker. Where does she get those perfect features," she reflected; "it must be from her own mother's side." And when alone in her room at last, Helen looked intently at her own face in the looking glass, beholding the dust on her eyelashes. Kind fate had made it a level, well cast glass, which reflected young Helen faithfully. And, when she had washed and dried her tender face into a glow, she asked herself concerning her open brown eyes, now luminous with youth and health, her delicate white skin and ears of porcelain kind—whether they were not as good as Lucy's. Morning and evening she gave praise that she had a little pleading mouth wherein were whitest teeth to bite with—level as the natural keys of a piano ; and on her head, the silkiest fawn coloured hair that ever was combed, thickly seamed with floss gold hairs. Helen's neck was so little round it could easily have been bitten in two, and she had not much of a chin. Still, though grieving at this now and then, she was never in tears about her looks—perceiving that she could hold her own. As she was popping on her little adornments, there came a soft knock at the door. This was Lucy. "Come in, darling," warbled Helen, getting ready to love Lucy much.

"Oh!" says Lucy, "I wanted to tell you. You must ring and make that idle Emma come to you whenever you want anything. She has nothing on earth to do for me till dressing time. How lovely your hair has grown, Helen."

" Yes, dearest," says Helen, kissing Lucy. " I'll ring."

" We'll have tea before long. I am sure you've had no luncheon, if the truth was known. Dear me, how lovely your hair looks done that way."

" Oh! how silly you are. I'm sure it's wretched hair. Who was that other lady sitting with aunt?"

" Oh! I forgot, you don't know any of the news. That's Miss Tresham"—the name brought the squire's terrible mistletoe story to poor Helen's memory—"she's so good natured and quaint. Her brother's here, too. He's rector of Norton Constantine, such a lovely place on the Wayfe—all belonging to him."

" Oh! indeed," said Helen, not wishing to display curiosity. " Where's Willie this vacation?"

" Oh! here; and I think he walked to Weald this morning to see the curate, who was at Balliol with him. He's reading so hard, dear fellow. Willie talks so often of George Newmarch, they're such friends."—There was a pause; whereupon

Lucy reproached herself, remembering that there had been a whisper of something, she had not cared to ask what. But she might have given pain. "I remember you had so many pets at Sawtry," she went on; "there was Bully—that hideous, delightful old dog."—

"Ah! I was so sorry to leave him."

"And your chesnut horse?"—

"Oh! Berty took her for a hunter."

"Do you see much of him now that he has become a Hussar?"

"Oh! no, not now," said Helen. She had been thinking all this time that no doubt Lucy viewed her as a great delinquent. What did she care? It was rather funny to be under the Rushworth ban, and they might all know that she had rowed to the island with George, if they liked. "Papa often sees Bertram in London," Lucy continued. "I suppose he has to go to escort the Queen?"

"I suppose so, poor fellow. He is so busy learning his drills, he never can get away for a day, he says. "I have seen most of Stephen," Helen explained—although she had an idea that Lucy did not believe her. "Isn't it a pity he stutters so. He has such queer cool ways, too, as if he didn't care for anyone."

"Oh! I like, Stephen," said the other. "Do you know, next year, Aunt Blanche is going to present me, and take me everywhere with her, now that she has no grown up daughter of her own, poor thing! If mamma doesn't go to London, I'm to stay in Charles Street with them. But I don't care much for it somehow."

Thought Helen 'George is always in Charles Street. She will make him care for her I know. Because she has finer features than I have.' "Ah! I was never in London but once with your papa," she said, pensively. "Why! I've never been anywhere but to Sawtry and here, Lucy."

"Oh! but I have made up my mind Aunt Blanche must ask you, too, or I should not enjoy it I know. I'm sure I shall not care for going out every night—to hot rooms and strange people. Can you understand always living among people one hardly knows?"

But Helen shook her head; and then there was a pause. "I saw a Mr. Maxwell in London, I remember," said she, trying to recall that time; "did you ever see him. He was rather good looking. Has he ever been here since I left?"

Lucy turned reproachfully to her cousin, but

there was no trace of design in Helen's face.—
" How is my old friend, Mr. Curry ?" she asked.

"Oh! just the same. Uncle Brian teases him as much as ever about being fond of venison ; isn't it cruel of uncle? Did you hear about that 'fright.' Altisidora Curry, thinking Lionel Stacey was going to marry her? I *must* tell you what Lady Knaresborough said about it !"

" Well, never mind now, darling," said Lucy, gently. "Poor Altisidora is very kind to her blind sister you know. And after all, don't you think Nelly, there are wretched things enough in the world already without dwelling on vanity and weakness, when we can help it; don't you think so, darling? I believe you are taller than me. Stand up, Nelly."

'Thank's for your pretty lecture,' Helen sneered to herself. And then in came Cathy.— "Oh! Nelly, we're all to go for a ride, to-morrow," she cried. " Mr. Tresham says he'll take us. D'you know, we're not allowed to ride by ourselves now ! and Willie hates horses. I shall go mad and desperate if nobody takes me out riding. George Newmarch was noble in those things. I love him for it, and I told him so."

" Uncle Brian scolds George because he

doesn't care so much for riding and hunting now," said Helen.

"Fancy!" Cathy ejaculated, "What would uncle Brian say tho', if George was like Willie— who won't even turn his head to look at the hounds when they pass, For my part I think brothers are horrid. Why, cousins are much better. And second cousins are best of all— they'll do anything for you."

This new table of consanguinity set Helen thinking. "Can Mr. Tresham ride across country?" she asked, proud of her familiarity with those subjects.

"Why, he's a clergyman," answered Cathy, laughing. "He's rather old."

"Cathy thinks forty quite a patriarch," Lucy said. "Mr. Tresham is my ideal. I could listen to him talking for ever. He has travelled everywhere, Nelly, and seen so much, and yet he never pushes forward what he knows and that,— unless you ask him to tell you. Ile was all through America and lived with a tribe of Comanches, or Apaches—oh! no *they'd* have eaten him—some red men."

"Yes, and Lord Hounslow told me he was made to take six wives," cries Cathy, "and he had to have their pet names tatooed all over him, none less than twenty-six letters long."

"Oh! Cathy—Cathy! How can that be true? When you know Lord Hounslow is always scoffing at good or earnest people," Lucy remonstrated. "Julia says her brother will never marry. If ever we may see a martyr it will be one like him, I think." Thus the three girls chatted away; adding subsequently whole pages-full of conversation on the subject of dresses, which, however, are omitted here.

Lady Penelope, of course, took possession of Helen at dinner time. She was far from easy in her mind just then about Mr. Curry's soundness on a certain great question of that day, and Helen, who was desperately hungry, had to answer for him on two or three points, and to keep on recalling bits of the last six months' sermons at Sawtry. Lady Penelope could never, she said, feel that her brother-in-law was quite safe—while that dead ministration continued in his Parish Church. Lucy and Mr. Tresham kept to themselves, talking away quietly all that evening. Next morning, however, Helen got a better view of this visitor while he read family prayers to them. There sat the three girls in their habits;

Lady Penelope seeming to sleep, and the servants —with stiff backs, and faces soaped and stolid— round the room. Helen, with that gift which has wisely been bestowed on ladies, of seeing without looking, remarked that he might have been handsome once, and was now rather old, and formidable on the whole, and that he read very clearly and beautifully. Then they had to turn round to kneel and pray.

After breakfast they were to ride to Draycote Abbey. It was seven miles off, but the road all the way has soft turf at either side to canter upon, and you can touch the blossoms of shady apple trees with your hand in many places. Lucy contrived to ride with her sister, for she had settled that Helen and Mr. Tresham ought to make friends as soon as possible, hence they were left together. But he was a stranger, and gentlemen were somewhat terrible to Helen, for, while plenty of thoughts were in her little head, she had not that art of taking a reckless header into conversation, which comes of seeing new people, in new places continually. He in his turn considered for some subject which would suit a shy young lady like this.

"Are there pretty rides near Sawtry?" he asked, quietly.

"Oh! yes, very," said Helen, blushing and twitching her little mouth into a look of trouble. "There's Chartloe Park and Monksylver," she added, at the cost of much trepidation.

"I was there a long time ago, I remember," said he. "My sister knows it well. She used to stay there."—

' Indeed she used,' thought Helen, and therefore blushed again. And, if she were going to continue the practise, this would be a most difficult young lady to talk to. Yet what a singular grace and attraction there was about her. "I remember the lake," he went on, "and Mr. Newmarch fishing from a punt. He was a famous fisherman, was he not?"

"Oh! yes; he taught me to catch a pike once," said Helen, laughing, for a change; and then Mr. Tresham noticed how frank and innocent her smile was. "You do not think fishing cruel?" he said, not knowing exactly what to say next.

"It was a little, little pike," she explained.

And he concluded, ' This is a mere child.'—

"Now shall we have a canter?" he asked, looking back for the others to follow. But if Helen ever looked pretty, it was galloping along, her head thrown back, and a laugh upon her face, despite herself—sitting there so graceful, so full of life. And steady, too, as a statue ; hands down, as George had taught her to carry them.—

"You must tell us that legend about the Abbey we're going to, remember," said Lucy, coming along side of them. And when they pulled into a walk next, he told the story, rather absently, though with a pleasant voice . . . . . . .
"and did he never come back from Palestine, after all ?" asked Lucy, at the end.

"Yes, to die, and to be buried at Drycote. His tomb ought to be there, I think. The very last of the race," he said. His thoughts, may be, wandering off to another beautiful churchyard, waiting for some one, also the last of his race, who might be coming in a little while.

It was a hot summer's day, and there was no wind to blow the branches about. The Abbey is down in a hollow, where many trees which the monks planted are still growing, and you hear no noises whatever save the cawing of rooks up aloft.

"The woman at the lodge will give us luncheon, I know," said Lucy; and then they found some one to hold the horses, and wandered about the Abbey buildings and round the dwelling house.

Mr. Tresham was charmed with the place. He pointed out the plan and remains of the different rooms to Helen, and she made a good listener, even if she were not much the wiser.

The woman of the place now came and took them to see what was indeed the old refectory. It remained intact, and in modern times had been consecrated for service.

"It was the oldest church in England," she told them. And Mr. Tresham had not the heart to contradict her.

After that, she led the way to the site of what had really been the former Abbey Church, whereof there remains but the base of one or two columns in the nave, and lifting up a wooden hutch in the turf, she shewed them the remains of a tesselated pavement there. "This is where the high altar stood," she explained.

"How came there to be two churches so close to each other, I wonder?" Mr. Tresham asked, mildly.

But the woman reminded them that one was a

Catholic and the other a Protestant Church. And when she said that, Helen looked at Mr. Tresham with a twinkle of fun in her eyes, expecting him to laugh, but he only looked on the ground. "No wonder they agreed to differ in this lovely place," he said, quietly.

"Yes, sir, they did. And here's where their conduit came out. They had to fetch their water in pipes from top o' yon hill, and there ain't no water like it the country round. Taste some out o' the coop, Miss."

But it was so cold Helen was afraid, till Mr. Tresham took some to encourage her. When the old woman was got rid of, they wandered about the ruins and grounds ; and by and bye sat under a great elm on the side of the hill, looking down on the house and the ruins.

"It almost makes me unhappy to be here," said Lucy ; "so much beauty, and so much more that is vanished and buried now. To think that all these people's work, and all they intended, is lost altogether for us."

She considered that the age of faith had fled for ever, she said.

"Yet, Thomas Cromwell gave a shocking account of this very place, I think," Mr. Tresham observed. 'Were young ladies' opinions really of much value on those questions?' he asked himself. He was a little tired of argument, too. Now, Miss Mallorie had no hobbies. Then Lucy, in reply, thought Cromwell hardly a fair informant—he had an object, as every one knew.

Meanwhile, Cathy and Helen were talking in a subdued way.—

"Would you like to be a nun, Nelly?—I'd like to be anything here."

"I'm sure I'd try to run away," Helen answered. "I should fear to be buried alive, like the poor nun in 'Marmion.'"

"But she was a wicked nun," interrupted Lucy. "No one could ever say that of you, Nelly."

"I don't know," said she, thoughtfully; and Mr. Tresham, overhearing them, decided that it would be hard to find a tribunal capable of condemning that child. Indeed, he watched her instead of the view before them. She interested him very much. An unusual look of suffering he, for his part, often noticed in her face, notwithstanding its youth; and in her timid eyes, a fixed and mournful expression.

Thus easily the summer's forenoon passed by.

The shadows crept further out on the grass, and the plumes of foliage shone with a yellow lustre as the sun came down to a level with them.

When the riders were hungry they went to the lodge and got bread and cheese. And a pretty group Lucy, and Cathy, and Helen made seated round the table in their trim blue habits. They stood up while he said Grace—three bright girls full of health and innocence. "Amen," Lucy and her sister said distinctly to his Grace. Helen moved her little lips with the same sweet intent.

It was a somewhat quaint idea—having charge of three young ladies thus. Thought he, ' At forty, one is past being much in awe of young ladies in their teens.' They had their talk, the three chatting away about everything, and he fell into a musing fit looking at them. He noticed how the place had given them new ideas, and how they could not arrange them readily, and were content to leave a thought quite incomplete if it led them at all far.

It was still and sunny outside : near the window sat Lucy, her back to the light, while the sun, threading through the leaves of some creeping plants, sparkled about the edge of her glossy hair and made a fringe of light around her head.

Lucy's voice proceeded calm and measured in his ears. One knew she would say her say without halting. On the other hand, when Helen spok e— she had only a twopenny question, or a laugh to add. Hers were little adjectives, learnt from nurses almost; verbs that one hears employed all day long. Her voice, too, was a foolish, appealing, child's voice. Yet to each long drawn sound one had to listen somehow with all one's ears, wondering what the speaker would think of next. Wasn't it Madame de Stael who had said that, to be pretty, she'd give all her wit and all her fame in exchange—to have people eagerly follow her face with their eyes, and grow abashed and tender when they talked to her? There was much in that, after all. It was well to be forty and wise, but one wearied of striking the balance for ever and ever in this wise. His reverie had indeed carried him away to foreign grounds.

Rushworth in those times was the quietest place to be found. Lady Penelope did not come downstairs till luncheon time, and people were left to do just as they liked during the morning. The girls, indeed, went to and fro from their mother's room with innumerable mes- sages—or enquiries about servants—or as to what

was going on in the school or at the farm.  Miss
Tresham wrote her letters in the library at this
hour.  She had a host of gossips and correspon-
dents, from whom she received all the news,
upon thick paper, stamped with the monograms
in vogue in that day.  Willie Felton was generally
reading, all by himself, and Mr. Tresham was
left alone.

"The Balfours want us to go to them,
Charles," said his sister to him one morning.

He considered a little before he spoke.  "Do
you know, Julia, I'm getting very lazy about
rushing hither and thither," he answered.  "The
Balfours have such *levées* always."

She looked at him, asking herself what could
be the idea behind all this.  "Not at this time of
year, Charles, I'm sure," she said.  "We can't
quarter ourselves on Penelope for ever.  And to
tell the truth, I begin to be a little tired here.  Is
the door shut?"—He did not care to look, tapping the window pane with his glove button.—
"You are wretched in London, you know, even
were my house ready to go into.  I'm sure
I'd make an effort and go to Norton if it were
possible, but Hugginson positively forbade it.
You know what he said, ' Miss Tresham, it was

the damp of trees at Liverbury, and nothing but those trees, that killed poor Sir Augustus Hippo.' I know it's not fair to ask you to cut timber near the house, and I would do anything to meet your wishes, Charles."—

He did not offer to cut down the trees.—"I want Lucy to come with me later in the year," she went on. "But I did not think of a party, of course."

"Ah! yes," he said at last, altogether ignoring the hint. "You included her cousin too, I suppose? I mean, Miss Mallorie?"

What was all this? It was not credible that her brother meant to make her unhappy. True she had often longed that he would change his mind about marriage—and there had been that eldest Miss Harlowe, at Pau last winter. But he had laughed then, at the bare mention. Now this child—with her little prettiness and her want of manner and her absurd age, and her uncertain prospects—it was incredible. Surely her duty was plainly to be most firm with her brother. "No, I have not included Miss Mallorie if you ask me, Charles. I think the girl very amiable of course; but very little manner, and altogether unpresentable."

He started; evidently she was right to be firm.

"Cruelly  narrow and harsh, I think," he said, impatiently.

"I am extremely careful in forming new friendships, I own, Charles.  Oh! dear me.  I can't feel interested in Miss Mallorie; really I've no patience!  Why does she  simper and call Lady Penelope 'aunt.'  Let me see.  Her mother's sister married Penelope's  brother."—

But when she said that much she quickly wished it unsaid, for her brother with an ominous frown upon his  face left the window, and biting his lips, commenced to walk from one end of the room to the other.  "Ha! very well, no doubt you're right," he said, and at each turn he got paler and paler.  Finally he stopped, and restraining himself with a  great effort, said—"Look, Julia; I was sure you would have liked and been kind to so blameless a person, for—my—sake," he added, trembling.  Then putting his hand with tenderness on his sister's shoulder.  "Have we ever quarrelled?" he asked, looking away and afar off, as if to review the years that were gone.  "Never, I think.  I sought always your happiness, wasn't it so, Julia?  Now I think very highly—very often—of Miss Mallorie," and when he had slowly made that speech, they both heard each other breathing.

And she had understood him; and knew all by degrees. So, to this it had come! Had she not lived in Curzon Street, within at least earshot of the very world, and seen how things go—too long to be deceived now. Her brother Charles! And then she thought how King David and King Solomon had both been deceived by women. There was no advantage in attempting to shut her eyes to the truth any longer. These things ever began in one way—and ended but in one way. "Oh!" she said, at first firmly. "I have no voice, I allow," but he did not seem to notice her, so occupied was he. What bitter things she thereupon said to him. She reminded him of their years of affection and confiding intercourse. Spoke of herself and her sisterly care for him. Humbly withal; but could he deny that she had been the best of sisters? She held up before his eyes, his moderation of judgment and self control hitherto; and then, though she, answering for him, made every allowance, there was little to be said in defence.—

But in reality all this time there had been perfect silence. Mr Tresham kicked feebly at a fray in the carpet as he passed it in his walk. Miss Tresham had said all these eloquent and scathing things to herself—with expressive twitchings of the lips and nothing else; holding the window curtain in her hand and fiddling with the braid on it. Who is not desirous to avoid the wordy carnage of a regular scene? There being still a dead silence, and neither being used to high words, the thing was put off to be talked over by and bye—as the most weighty things are—by those unused to strife, because of the pain of them; and Miss Tresham went to her own room. Her brother had given her a cruel shock. What would Penelope say, first of all? What would this person say, and that? But it was altogether overwhelming, and, in the solitude of her own room, she began to cry bitterly.

And for her brother, left alone, the dread was that somebody would come and talk to him—Lucy or Lady Penelope. But not a sound was to be heard, save a gardener whistling now and then in the garden. It was summer; and sometimes he heard a man sharpening his scythe outside, and the noise of birds spinning from shrub to shrub. At last he looked carefully at the clock. It was half-past twelve, so he went out.

## CHAPTER VIII.

THE little Helen sat by a pond at the top of the garden under the orchard wall. The banks of the pond were of turf and finished off smooth and sleek, like the rim of a vase, and the whole place was tended with great care. By the pond was a little thatched summer house, kept clean as a pin; the floor laid out with pebbles, in a pattern, black and white; seats were all round. But Helen preferred to sit on the dry turf at the edge of the pond. As she peered into the water in search of a fish, three tame ducks floated up to her and enquired for crumbs.

"I have nothing to give you," said Helen, shaking her head sorrowfully.

George could always see a fish in the water, but she never could. How he used to discover trout, ever so far off! As for the ducks, they circled off with no opinion of Helen. What had she to give, that any one thought worth having?

And deeming herself insignificant, she fell to musing. No one troubled themselves about her at all! Perhaps *he* did once; but had he not laughed and sneered on the island? Queer, that she should begin to think about it that day! He made fun of her, and Lady Adelaide said things afterwards that were frightful. She sighed several times. Heaven would take care of her if she were deserted; but it took care of Lucy and Catherine much more nicely.

She said she was beginning to forget Sawtry now. It was, after all, a long, long time since she had lived there—ages! Luncheon and dinner and bed-time are sure to come every day, whatever happens; and readings with Lady Penelope, and practising and taking walks, repeat themselves. Her mind got into a groove; there were these things to look forward to every morning and evening—little duties and interests. Truly she had become used to Rushworth.

Some one's step sounded on the walk.

"Who can this be?" Helen wondered. "A man's walk—and with thin boots, too! If it is Willie, I shall have fun teasing him—if he's come to read, for he's always good tempered."

But when she looked up it was Mr. Tresham.

# CHAPTER XI.

.

" Rushworth Park,
"Ricehope.

" My dear Sister,

"It is long since I sent you three
sermons of the Bishop of Saint Dunstan's. You
have taken no notice of them. Had I leisure,
there is much, very much, to take exception to in
your comments on that sad question of the Boreall
Magna Decision, but not time this post. Charles
Tresham has intimated to me his proposals made
to marry our niece, Helen Mallorie (this yesterday)—and your surprise, I am convinced, will
equal my own. I have reflected that you had
more control over the girl than myself, and after
giving it a night's thought, I write to you at
once. You know Charles Tresham slightly, and
his sister well, I think. The property I under-

stand to be five thousand a-year. The family, you know, is one of the very best in the south of England, and this is the last of them. He is anxious, we conclude, that this should be provided against, and Julia and I have often wondered that steps were not taken before. The sister, poor thing, is not *écharnée* for this alliance, but the brother's mind is made up unalterably. Our dear girl, of course, saw her duty at once in a proper spirit. Nothing could exceed his nobleness and liberality on the subject of settlements, as far as I permitted myself to enter into his plans; but those were, I said, matters on which I begged to refer him to Brian and yourself for details. I think it is our part to feel very grateful to Providence that this marriage has been decided upon by its all-wise decrees. I venture to give no opinion myself as to the wisdom of Mr. Tresham's choice. My opinions, doubtless, would not weigh with you or anyone. My boy Willie returns, of course, to Christ Church. He is well, with my girls. Julia Tresham sends her very kindest regards to you and Brian, but no doubt she is writing as well.

"Your affectionate sister,

"PENELOPE FELTON."

It was in this fashion announced to Lady Adelaide that her little girl, who had left only a fortnight ago, was to be Mr. Tresham's wife.

When he found her all alone, staring into the water, he had hardened his heart to ask her to marry him, and to his words of tenderest respect she had listened with a great fluttering of awe and bewilderment. Not without long meditation and many hours of questioning had he taken such a step ; and as fruit of such reflection, he was very sure that this was the only woman he had ever wished with all his heart to make his Wife. Surely by no other standard but his own experience could the wisdom of that decision be judged. Long he had lived, and had learned to bring a clear and steady insight to bear on every question that he met, and it was time that he should claim to answer to himself alone for a choice such as this. And his sister, we had seen, was at first very angry, and then very sad, for she loved her brother more than anything in the world. But a reaction came, and now, having no iron will to put in motion, she would not obstinately harden her face and declare her own judgment infallible. From habit, she was eager rather to submit to her brother. When, therefore, he sought her later in the day, and told her very simply what he had done, and asked to be forgiven if he had pained her at all—pouring out all his heart indeed— what could she do but wish him well and promise to love Helen dearly for his sake?

Hence there had been no coldness or warfare between Miss Tresham and Helen. The elder lady was, perhaps, at all times somewhat dry and hard to interest; but then she was one of those people who would sit and talk to a person for hours without showing whether she was greatly pleased or repelled by them. May be that Helen detected little affection for herself. But that discovery, if ever made, was funded in the innermost corner of her heart, and she was modestly silent when the good lady sought her out to congratulate her—repeating to Helen, with many kisses, that she would never know what a treasure Providence was giving to her.

Lucy Felton was startled and vaguely frightened by all these things at the first. And something whispered to her that there was danger ahead. But when she calmly thought it all over,

' He is far wiser than I,' she said. " Perhaps *he* sees and knows what is hid from me."

And so, if she recognised a temptation to doubt

and suspect Helen, she would begin the more
now to help her all she could. When her mother
sent for her, late at night, therefore, it was Lucy's
task to lessen her astonishment and misgivings.
The elder lady could not be sure of Charles Tresham's sanity even, and it took all her daughter's
temperate words and subtle excuses to soften
Lady Penelope's anger. When once she had
made up her mind that this marriage was not
wrong and was his wish, this downright girl set
herself to forward it in every way she could.
She saw that Mr. Tresham avoided meeting her
in the evening of that day, and she made elab-
orate excuses for him, longing for the next morning, that she might tell them both how glad
she was. Arguing thus, on the eventful night,
Lucy's thoughts and prayers blended quietly into
sleep.

Helen was all day oppressed with fear. She
hoped that the feeling would go away ; but it never
went. This was a day passed in obscure thoughts.
The rooms were hot and beautiful, it being a
summer's afternoon. She went from one to the
other for change. She used not to dare to go
into the drawing-room without leave, once.
Fortune, power, and contentment were now com-

ing to her. To be the wife of a rich and clever
man : this was inevitable. Now and then she took
a sip at such reflections. Afterwards she walked
hither and thither again. Her lover came to her
at times. Then Cathy came—much awed; and
she had to see Miss Tresham in the way related
above.

Night seemed to make its appearance without
warning. She would begin to think when the
morning came, she resolved; so went away to bed.
The mutinous blood did keep lapping up against
her little brain, and she was worn out and sorry
for herself. In this mood slipped off into a deep
sleep. For a few hours she slept without turning.
But of a sudden, with a twist or two, Helen was
wide awake—in a room intensely dark. She tossed
her white arms, and as consciousness by degrees
stirred each coiled up thought into motion—
' What had happened ? ' she asked. Something
waited to be remembered. It was his declaration.
But was not that a supreme triumph, and real ?
She had not this instant made it up from the
shreds of old dreams. In the early day, when it
was light, he had offered to her. A proud
thought. Nevertheless, she was shuddering. As
of old—sorrow, with unfortunate face turned—

attended by her bed head. And then, without any choice, she was on the subject of George Newmarch. Straightway she saw into his college room—where there was no one but he, frowning and trying to snatch at his thoughts, as he was wont. "He frowns," said she, " when I look at him." In the quiet room of this lone house Helen felt currents of fear pass over her heart. Perhaps she had done a fatal thing. She sat up and tried to see some object, through the woolly darkness, that would reassure her. "They will trouble me," she said, thinking dejectedly of him and his sorrows. Now she knew for the first time the grievous yearning which comes, to be able to go back and undo that which has been done; to beat open the heavy doors locked behind us. But she was young and well, and reaction came. By and bye she felt herself laughing gently. Had he ever cared for her at all? was she doing him any wrong, save in her own foolish mind? She had always cried over her story books and was sorry for the heroes—they never troubled her afterwards. When it was light she would not see George Newmarch frowning again. What grandeur was promised to her. She might think of pleasant things for hours, and yet not have finished them all then. She was going to be in love and be loved, as it seemed, systematically with the ceremonies prescribed—not on a lake. Not on a poor lake.

How generous he was, and how devoted, and how noble. What ought she to have said? She knew not; then she remembered how simple and guileless she had felt and looked—standing like a lamb. She thought of her manner with admiration. And—a laugh on her face—Helen fell asleep again.

Threading through the figures of our story, let us go back to Lady Adelaide, who had just heard of this. Recognising her sister's writing, she had put the letter by at first. Penelope's long essays were somewhat of a tax. Peremptory letters of other kinds awaited her in plenty, and her boys claimed all the time and thought she could find. Who could be expected to dissect the Bishop of St. Dunstan's charges? They bore their own refutation on the face of them, only too plainly. Would the government never interfere to remove offences? But what came in the next sentence? All Berty's wildness and George's sorrows vanished from her mind, as she read through every word of those three letters from Rushworth, and when they were thoroughly known, Lady Adelaide rose and went in search of her husband, eager to tell him and have his good wishes. He sat in his great arm chair, before the library fire-place; on the table behind him, a number of bills and letters. And from the reading of these his face had gathered a look of weary anger—common in those days. "Well, I've been married to you now for twenty-nine years," he said, slowly, not looking up, "and you've never learnt that difficult thing yet, my Lady Adelaide. Did I tell you the story about Dean Swift and his servant, now?"

Doubtless it had often been told. When Lady Adelaide *had* shut the door, therefore she began,

"Dear Brian—can you listen? our—my precious girl is to be married!"

"Going to be, did you say?" the Squire said, not turning round. "Well, didn't I always tell you? Now was that what my son George went to stop with Lady Blanche for?"

"Brian!!" said his wife. "Pray listen and try to spare me. Yes, indeed Brian, I have heard this moment that Charles Tresham —" The Squire gave a long sigh, which died away into a groan. "Charles Tresham has made dearest Helen an offer of marriage. For my part I think it is very desirable. She never gave me a day's real anxiety in my life. I feel as if I loved her like one of my own—I am sure she will be happy, Brian. I think the fatherless and the orphan are always cared for; I never knew it otherwise," and here she sobbed, and coming near, she took her husband's hand, which was very cold. He said nothing. "Is is not so?" said Lady Adelaide. "He writes such a noble letter. Will you read it? It is a wonderful future for my girl. His must be a fine property. I don't know how to be thankful enough for the sweet child's sake. Brian, you say nothing?"

"Give it here!" said the Squire, thinking of the letter; which shook so that he could not read far.

Lady Adelaide went on, "You will read Julia's also. Do not refuse. I think as far as they go into particulars, nothing could be nobler. My precious girl will be independent for the rest of her life, Brian," said she, for his eyes were fixed upon the curly paper in the grate, and he seemed to fear something. "Brian, dare I oppose what my conscience tells me is for the child's own happiness and advantage? Child! they were both children. That is all over. Why did you not speak before if you thought of that? Can I say I think she will be unhappy? Would I wish that at any price?"—and she began thereupon to muse, looking far and away, through the walls and to the vague beyond. " No, no," said Lady Adelaide, " I for my part am very happy and very glad."

Said he, "Oh! Adelaide!" But what he did mean, and why he cared, no one ever knew. While she stood with grave face, attending him and growing more assured each minute in her own mind, that she was right, he only said, " I'll write. Ask them all to come here. Well, what do I know about 'em all?"

Perhaps this was as much as one could expect. She needed not to go into the question of her husband's strange manner, or to notice it at all. The dear child was not thinking of anyone else even. Where would half the world be, if all flirtations of a week were to be graven in stone? something to that effect she repeated. What could shew more want of right judgment, or indeed be more impious, than to oppose and thwart all Helen's hopes and prospects now? She settled this decisively, and then, walked a little—and had to argue about it all over again. The postman had to wait at the gate till the last moment that evening for the Rushworth letters, each of them trebly crossed, and dashed with loves and congratulations. All the Rushworth party were to come to Sawtry, before long, Helen at once, if *some one* could spare her; that some one whom Lady Adelaide would henceforward look upon as best and nearest friend. Then she wrote a short note to Lord Newbury, the first no doubt for many years ; and finally, in great charity with all men, sat down and studied the Bishop of St. Dunstan's last charge. There were many, she remembered, who called this, perhaps, ill-advised Prelate, a large hearted, and truly spiritually-minded man.

There was thus an altogether disproportionate fuss and disturbance made about a little girl of this sort, with hitherto, no prospects. But somehow every one discovered that they were fond of Helen ; nor could one word or act be remembered against her from the first hour of her coming there. Being kind hearted people, all the household were glad, and to some it was a change from the constant raw open on account of Berty's and George's follies. No one thought much about

George.   It was Stephen, after all, who informed him of what had happened.   His letter to London related—that it was awful slow at home, since he had come from school.   Old Pringle had declared that he had no clothes left in the world, save blue flannel shirts, too small for him,  and white ties ; and  that  he  had  grown  a  rod  taller.   Lord Knaresborough  had  quarelled  with  his  keeper, who was going  to  Obonbury.   Traylen had shot one of the Muscovy  ducks  with  a  rifle,  because papa said  he  couldn't  hit  it.   Reginald Stacey was going to Cambridge  next term.   And at the end it mentioned that Helen was going to  marry a chap called Tresham, a parson, with lots of tin— a very good fellow, and awfully spoony on Helen.

George once vowed never to darken his uncle's door again.   But searching his heart so painfully —and getting so much  inward light of  late, he had forgotten that pledge.   Mr. Ellis had written a kind letter to him, full of good advice, bidding him be of good cheer, and  to  make  a  fresh start from this out.   So he went to London, where he communed much and  gloomily  with  himself in those days.

It made no difference at Sawtry, whether he went or stayed.   The Squire was wearing out his heart about Berty's career. To paying of bills for the spoilt young prince there was already no end. Mr. East, the family lawyer, had been to see Berty in London, and said he seemed to be going on—just anyhow; yet the boy had enchanted him, too; swinging—to use a figure—his censer of fun and high spirits—filling his rooms at Strong's Hotel, where he was to be found in great state, with laughter and light. He was the handsomest boy that had ever been seen about London; and he never told a lie, or said one thing when he wanted another done. His face was as white as a lily, and he had the brow and eyes of a prince; yet he had no pride and would make friends with servants—or with the poorest and most wretched people, obliging every one he met to be as merry as himself.

These were gilded days of eternal hansoms and smiling waiters. And silks—silks eternal. Finely coloured hair; and parasols, and broughams to drive him about. The most dangerous set of men also took Berty up, and launched him in the middle of the stream.

His colonel and the captain of his troop, and the drill instructors and riding masters, spoilt him from the first day. He could never, somehow, find time to go to Sawtry; but he lived, almost, at Strong's Hotel, and he would have a special train to any Race that was going on, should he lie in bed too late in the morning. His delicately cut features and shining satin hair, were to be seen in the window of a well-known library and Print Shop that year. It was a group—he and the young Earl, or Duke, or Marquis, then most in vogue —each with a race glass—supposed to be encouraging those open air sports in which we are unrivalled as a nation.

If men let Berty have his own way, what treatment did the other caste accord him? Broken hearts truly strewed the various Provincial towns where his Regiment, or Detachments from it, happened to be quartered. He had an inveterate habit at this time of engaging himself to be married—at a ball, or archery party, or on the top of a drag after a luncheon. At Halifax, Pontefract, and Leeds, his nuptials with young ladies of the society there had been announced. And in the great Hardware Metropolis he had proposed for and been accepted by, two sisters, successively, in the family of a leading Fork and Electro-Plate manufacturer; as they had both been engaged at the time to be married elsewhere, it created some stir. But when the Regiment marched away to Manchester, Berty, in truth, forgot the whole thing; and as he had always cut the other members of the family, never remembered any of them again. He was now engaged to the only child of a Cotton Spinner, of enormous wealth, in the neighbourhood of Burnley, where his troop was on detachment at this time. They were to wait, however, till he was twenty-one.

Helen came from Rushworth ten days or so after Lady Penelope's letter. She was so glad to be at dear old Sawtry again; she talked to everyone, and patronised them. She had grown ever so much older. She was twice as beautiful. She carried herself as easily and discreelty as people of twice her years.

And when the others arrived Miss Tresham's coming made the Squire a young man again, he said. They had, it appeared, been wont to flirt pertinaciously with each other, when the century was much younger, and the Squire declared that Julia's attractions made Lady Adelaide cruelly jealous to this day. He also liked to pay Helen marked homage since her promotion. He would watch with cynical curiosity for symptoms of female vanity and pretensions on the young lady's part; but there was little to be read in that tranquil and plaintive face, and he had to hold his peace, falling back on the firm consolations of his own scepticism.

The ladies in those days so usurped the situation that there was danger of Helen's head being turned; for every one in the country knew who the Treshams were, and people came to call on Helen, or rather to look at the future mistress of Norton Constantine.

Mrs. Stacey too, made a point of sending Helen a gracious message. ' She regretted that Lady Adelaide and she did not see each other, but hoped to know Helen better ; for some of her happiest hours had been spent at Norton, as a girl, and she and Charles Tresham had been almost children together.'   This cut both ways.

Lady Knaresborough came, too, and she, as indeed did all visitors, learnt from Helen's few artless words, that it was she who had yielded to the fervour of Mr. Tresham's devotion, instead of seeking the alliance in any way.

The only unconcerned person at Sawtry was Stephen.   If no one noticed him, he certainly did not put himself out for anybody.   The leaves were beginning to turn a bit now, and the grass on the islands was not so fresh and glittering as in early June. He had his own devices to occupy him, fishing all day, or keeping up the rowing muscle acquired on the Thames. Helen thought sometimes that he was unkind not to take her out riding oftener. He also objected to galloping on hard ground. " It was only women," he grumbled, " who wanted to ' bucket' horses in summer. Girls would go and break down the largest stable of horses in England in a week, if they were let."

But he respected Helen, too, because Mr. Tresham now belonged to her; and because she was ascending, as it were, into the higher tier of governors and relations, and the like.

One beautiful day Helen asked him to row her up the lake. ' Something had been lost,' she said, to herself, ' since she rowed with one of her cousins last.' It was hot and still, and the black and white cows and calves on the bank looked up at them from out of the high gold and green grasses—shaking off the flies. The rowlocks creaked to the oars' going; ' and,' thought she, ' the way we break the water frightens these poor swifts and martens from getting their flies.' For the insatiable birds came and went, and stopped, and shot up off the water in clear curves, whipping the lake and the blue sky which took a bath in it, with cross bars of shadow.

She would row at Norton; not with these three boys, for she would have to mind the servants and the visitors. Stephen was a stranger. When she watched the swifts, her eyes would blink—though now she had as many parasols as she desired, no doubt. *He* had promised her one once—when she should go to Commemoration.

"I wonder where he is now," she said, aloud.

Stephen having nothing to say, remained silent. And lying down to his work, quickly sculled to the top of the lake. "Where d'you like to go?" asked he.

"Oh! I don't know; let us gaze about us here. How lovely it is; is it not, Stephen?"

He was looking down into the water, and rapping the stretcher with his toes.

"You never have a word to say to me now, Stephen. I believe I've offended you. Have I? I think you never cared for any one, did you?"

"Eh?" said he, wondering what she wanted. "No; did you? Oh! but I forget: I beg your pardon." He considered her rather a bore. Did she want to know  if he, too, thought of being married?

" Take me to that island," she said—chagrined because this dry, hard boy was so unlike some one she had rowed with once.   Had he nothing to say to amuse her  even?   There was *one* who trembled when  he  looked at  her  gloves.   Tiff wrenched the  boat  round, and  making for  the island, landed her in a few seconds.

' It is beautiful here.  And it is my own place,' said she, to herself, and went to the spot where they  had sat upon that summer afternoon.

" What  an  odd  place  to  admire,"  said Tiff, who remained holding the chain belonging to the boat in his hand, and watching  her  roaming  to and fro.  ' She had got awfully conceited,' he said. It is certain that they kept no one waiting dinner for them  that afternoon.

In due time Mr. Tresham came to Sawtry also, and the love making progressed  in  set fashion. Everything  was  encouraging ;  Heaven  itself seemed to smile on their wooing, it was observed. The  Squire  abstained  from  making  any very dreadful remarks, for he had taken a liking to the lover.   The next few weeks passed,  therefore, very happily.   Helen made the most dutiful of lady loves; ever ready to walk when he was, and to go in about the time that Lady Adelaide recommended.   It was noticed that she got prettier every day, and an increasing tinge of reserve and dignity improved her in everyone's judgment. As he came to know her, she won his admiration and esteem more and more.   With delight he beheld her character develope under his eye.   If he had dreaded at times in his inmost heart that she whom he loved so earnestly might prove herself childish and unformed, beyond the first impression even, he found, when he knew her better, that it was far otherwise.   Indeed, when she learnt to talk to him with more confidence, he found that his affianced bride had a prim vein of satire of her own, and enjoyed a delicate appreciation of other people's faults that had much of mental promise about it.   He would persuade himself to humour this pretty spice of malice, since it amused her; though to him such a turn of mind was quite a novelty. It is to be supposed she saw how that was, too, after a while, for they never once had a quarrel or contradiction.

While the pair in whom all were interested were studying each other's character in their own way, Miss Tresham and Lady Adelaide became close friends—the elder lady confiding her anxieties and longings for her boys to the other. She wished Stephen to have a Commission, she thought, and that in some gentlemanly Corps, where there was no gambling and no sin; but for these there were many applicants, and vacancies were rare, she understood.

If her opinion were asked, Miss Tresham would recommend getting the ear of THE DUKE—(not the Duke, though in those days, also, it was a duke who ruled)—but Lady Adelaide shook her head. "And of course," Miss Tresham suggested, "you have spoken to Lord Henry." (This was many, many years ago.)

"Dear me! I've only seen him once. Would he be of any use?" said Lady Adelaide, in rather a maze. "If I had only known! He took me in to dinner the other night, at Chartloe."

"My dear, *the* very man," explained Miss Tresham, who, as we know, had lived long in Curzon Street and those parts of the Town, and not altogether in vain. "Can do anything—the Adjutant-General, my dear."

"What a pity! And I never thought of saying a word for my poor Stephen the other night. He seemed so good natured, too. I thought he

would have gone on his knees—spilled some
soup on my dress, and Lady Knaresborough told
him he was always—what was it?—on his knees
to everybody.  I forget."

Then they digressed to talking about their
neighbour's, Lady Knaresborough's, vagaries
and shortcomings; but the mother kept that hint
about Lord Henry in her mind.  'Would it not be
well,' she thought, 'if the great man could be
enticed by some means or other to Sawtry.'
"I know him," says the Squire, when she
spoke on the subject making short work of it.
"I'll ask him to come and shoot, if I don't forget
all about it."

This was in the last days of August, and it fell
out that one day when partridge shooting had
begun, Mr. Newmarch's party, walking up a piece
of stubble which joined Lord Knaresborough's
land, came upon four or five gentleman from
Chartloe, having luncheon under a shady knot of
trees in a corner.  If men can ever be friendly
and cheery, 'tis at a time like that.  The birds
had been plentiful and well behaved ; and the sun
shining out, raised everybody's spirits, while the
late rain had made the scent lie well in the swedes.
Mr. Newmarch did luckily remember to ask Lord

Harry to come over and shoot with him. There was a peculiar kind of long grass in Sawtry Park, wherein the birds lay famously; and besides, most of the leases on the Squire's land had a clause against reaping by machinery, so that his stubbles were of the old fashioned kind, and untouched, he said, this year as yet.

The cheery Horse Guards magnate was delighted to come, he declared; and, a couple of days later, drove over with Lord Knaresborough, in a hurry, of course, as he had to be in London that night.

There was not so easy going and good tempered an old bachelor in the service as Lord Henry. People called him Lord Harry, as if his very name had a jovial twang about it. Those who had had occasion to suffer it—declared that they would rather be 'blown up' by him, than talked to coolly by other people. As for Lady Adelaide, she thought him quite an angel in thus giving them a day—when his time must be so precious. She puzzled her simple head to anticipate what would be the best way of providing for or anticipating the tastes of her guest: but Miss Tresham, when she was appealed to, could not recollect to have ever heard that he was partial to anything specially beyond good dinners, pleasant men, agreeable women, and nice things of every sort. Fortunately, when Lord Harry did come, he took a decided fancy to Stephen, for whom it turned out a most eventful day—because he made a most wonderful shot.

It was in this wise. At the beginning, Stephen kept quite by himself—in a fit of lofty shyness not uncommon to him. But on the way to that part of the park where the dogs and keepers awaited him, Lord Harry, who had already suffered a little coaxing at Lady Adelaide's hands, began "So I hear you want to be a soldier, young gentleman, eh?"

"Yes, very much, sir," answered Tiff, not shaking off his reserve.

"Like this sort of thing—eh?" said his friend laughing, and putting his gun to his shoulder in a discursive fashion.

"I wanted to be in the army, certainly," said Tiff, without any design. "I don't know that I can shoot much though."

"That would be like old Augustus Wylcote, Newmarch," Lord Knaresborough suggested, "asking for a cavalry command in India, the other day, on the ground of being such a ' thruster ?' "

" Why, he can't walk I'm told," said the squire.

" I should think not, myself; but the Duke listened to him, and says he, ' are not you getting rather old for active service, General ?' ' Why I can beat all the young fellows at Melton still your grace,' said the old boy. Can't you fancy him! just after a tremendous luncheon at Poodles."

" And a pill," added Lord Harry.

" Cook told me about the regiment his son's in," said Stephen, taking courage. " His son ran away to enlist, and he's a corporal now. When they were at Mooltan, he says, they used to lie under wooden screens with their rifles and pick the Sikhs off at their guns. That was wonderful, I think."

" You seem very deep in Cook's confidence," said Lord Knaresborough.

Stephen laughed. " In the cub hunting I used to take him out cold partridge of mornings, and so I got into his graces that way," said he.

When they had been at work for about half an

hour, Stephen made his shot.  They happened to come, taking a steep field sideways, on a bit of a sheep pond with a few thorn trees growing round it.  The pond was on the slope of a hill under stubble; the banks shelved abruptly down to it on the top side, where Lord Harry's place was.  Now the water was exactly in front of Stephen's beat in line, and as he stood debating by which side to go round, up got a wildish covey a little to his left, across the pool.  Lord Knaresborough on Tiff's right fired and killed his bird; somebody else killed another; Lord Harry picked one out, but wasn't in a hurry.  Tiff who stood in rear of everybody, risked a long shot, and fired— almost amongst the trees—missed his bird clean, and his shot struck Lord Harry—who was half hid behind a thorn stump—in the leg.  He jumped up in the air, and Tiff thought he had broken his leg.  Every one ran up.  A few grains had actually gone through the General's trousers, and the skin was grazed.  Tiff was grievously sorry and ashamed, and said so as best he could.  But Lord Henry never lost his spirits and wouldn't hear of not going on at once. " 'Pon my honour, young gentleman," he said, examining his shins, with a comical face, " if you can't shoot better than that—why you must go into the Service and learn."

Indeed one would think he enjoyed the whole thing rather; anyhow it took a very great deal to put him out of temper.

" Lady Adelaide," he said therefore, when the day was over, " your boy has settled the question," And what a dear old man she thought him ! " Only," he added, " tell my young Eton friend that it's *directly* contrary to the Articles of War to make a target of your superior officer."

Nor did it turn out that he forgot his promise. For in a few days there came a nice thick letter from the Horse-Guards, saying that Stephen's name was down—in somebody's list somewhere, and would receive its due attention and so forth.

So Stephen had all the autumn to enjoy himself, with a pleasant prospect at the end of it. He and Mr. Tresham struck up a great friendship, and when no love-making was going on, they were close companions. By patient diplomacy, Tiff managed to evolve two rideable horses for the cub hunting. One was an ex-carr iage horse, who kicked; the other, a rough four-y ear-old from the farm. The plotting to get this latter animal singed and taken on the strength of the stable, was most delicate and trying; but with Neal's aid, it was at last managed. And no morning was too wet or raw to keep Stephen from finding out Cook and his young hounds among the woodlands; and, as·he never chattered or made a fuss, he steadily won Cook's gloomy approbation. Once they killed a cub, at seven o'clock in the morning, under the dining-room windows, at Sawtry; and Helen, looking out with sleepy eyes, saw Tiff, Cook, and one of the whips, silently watching the hounds break up their fox in the drizzling rain.

Meanwhile, poor George had spent the time, till term commenced at St. Abbs, with the Ellis's. Even now he was not able to go in for things with much spirit. Perhaps they ended by getting a little tired of him in Charles Street. The days were intolerably long and hot there. He fell upon old friends in London, of course; and being known to be under a cloud of some sort, might have had a certain amount of sympahty—such as is readily extended to a youth enduring the common lot, which his companions have a foreboding may be theirs by and bye.

He did not care, though, to meet men he had known at school or college, now that he was no-body—and good for nothing and doing nothing.

Once, in Bond Street, he actually came upon Algy Woodville—hanging on some fellow's arm, and in the best of after-luncheon spirits. De-lighted to see George—he gave him a cheery shake of the hand; and poor George, losing all presence of mind, had nothing ready made to say to him. So, like any other acquaintances, they passed on on their ways, and with a feeling of vexation and littleness, George looked back, and saw Algy's glossy hair and brilliant new hat—worn on one side—disappearing round a plate glass bend in the street, while, by degrees, ever so many things that he might have said kept coming into his head.

That wedding, George had been told, was to be in the following Spring. He was to go to Sawtry for it. It, to be sure, was something to look forward to. He had written a letter of congratulation to Helen; of course, he ought to do so. How lucky it was now that he had held his peace that afternoon on the island!

She was to be married in March, at Sawtry; and there was much to be thought of all the

Autumn. She had been to London for a while with Lady Adelaide, and the two ladies had stayed in Charles Street, from whence George had departed a few days before, to begin life at his dreaded college.

Mr. Tresham was sometimes at Sawtry, and sometimes at Norton—where much had to be done before it was fit to receive his bride. And Miss Tresham, forgetting her ague for a week or two, ran down there—unknown to Sir Mathew Hugginson, I suppose—to help.

The lovers were together at Christmas once more, and a happy, peaceful season it was that year, for them all. Then the early spring passed quickly away, and Mr. Tresham had to run up to London once before he came back to Sawtry for the event. "We are to be separated once more, Helen," he said, quietly, in the morning; "but not for long, I trust."

And she, as she always did, meekly hung her head and smiled ever so sweetly, with a few words of good-bye. How trusting and gentle she looked! and yet, when the peaceful smile was about her mouth, her thoughts were very busy.

She was sorry when he went. He used to think for her, and to keep her from incessantly going over old times, by his presence and his cheerful talk. She did not like to be thrown on herself.

The bridesmaids were chosen, and asked to be ready, and the wreaths selected, and the programme settled—by this. It wanted but a short time to the wedding day, and there was little more to be attended to. She dreaded leaving Sawtry; she had never known how dear it was till now, and that was what kept weighing on her spirits. There was a river at Norton Constantine, which Mr. Tresham had described to her. But no lake. And no islands, which were so beautiful. Often in those days she would pay certain dear old places a last visit, and her bull dog went with her as he used to do. Stephen would be away following the hounds whenever he could manage it. Whether or no, they had not much in common. But he was better than nothing.

One evening after she had submitted for hours to Mrs. Pringle's fussing over things that were being made, she walked out late on the chance of meeting her cousin coming back from hunting, taking the path he would have to return by. But the dew soon wetted her boots, and she wandered back to find a book to read till dinner time. The

hall was dark  when  she pushed open the  great
door and  slowly mounted  the staircase—whence
turning round, she stared about her.  A fog seemed
to possess the place.   The windows reared themselves—slabs of cold and  dusty light, and the
tiers of cases, and the pictures, huge and undefined
at this  hour, brought  trouble to  Helen's  mind.
There came once the distant noise of  a door shut-
ting, and  after a time began, from she knew not
where, slow musical sounds, rising and falling—
filling the air with wailing chords, all far off and
above her; each one an appeal to whatever is most
sad,  and  most easily  touched  in one's brain.
Walking slowly, Helen  followed  the music—not
sure now if she would ever find the cause of it—
into the drawing room, and heard it plainer there.
Pushed open the library door, and saw that it was
Lady Adelaide, who played to herself upon the
organ.   Helen stopped half in the doorway—lest
the sweet musician should pause.  But mylady
hearing the step, called Helen to her, and made
her kneel by the chair, glad  that there was no
light but twilight.  She  presented her cold face
to be kissed, saying, "How soon my girl leaves
me. I remember that it is only an hour since my
bird came to me first.  You know  I am always

thinking of you now. Not unhappily, sweet. But I think—"

"Do not sigh so."

"May I speak to you?"—Helen kissed her friend, which pretty sound was the only one to be heard for some time. "Yours has not been an attachment like that of many girls?"—Lady Adelaide asked gravely, while Helen's cheek touched her face. The girl strove to listen attentively, looking out at the dark garden, and at the trees bending and complaining to each other. In that solemn hour, she asked herself whither she was tending : but she whispered, without emotion in her voice,

"Why do you ask, aunt? He is so noble and good. We all love him, do we not?"

"Yes, my darling. But besides that, besides that, I do earnestly believe the happiest marriages in the world are such as yours. You are going to marry the truest, best, and kindest of Christian men and gentlemen. You will daily learn to respect and love him more and more. It will be built up every day, Helen, of your very happy married life."—Lady Adelaide sometimes sighed, sometimes saying prayers to herself. Helen was considering how she had began at the other end of the chain from people she had heard of—who, first love each other a great deal, and then want to marry each other, they think. She herself was so busy in the getting wed that she had not yet had the time to sigh for love. "Heaven will bless you," Lady Adelaide was saying, "for you are my own dear gentle child, and there is never anything worth having but His blessing, sweet. I wanted to tell you that—to hear you talk ; to be sure you were— happy. Only I knew that!" Helen was thinking again of the pretty house that she would have and the state and honour of it. Of the people she could ask to stay with her. She thought about Mr. Tresham, when he was with her. Because her child did not seem to wish to speak, Lady Adelaide asked if she might pray for her. So they knelt down. Helen prayed aside, hoping that the tale of the world being cruel and cold, and ungrate- ful, was no more true than other deterrent tales.

They would not call for lights even then, but sat in the darkness—Lady Adelaide's hand smoothing her pet's hair, over and over. She knew that sooner or later it must have come, and she must have parted with her. Hence- forth she would think of Helen as beyond care and disturbance. A girl who had ever kept

her sympathies and hopes to herself. Undemon-
strative; but where had there ever been a gentler
or more obedient one than this. How unlike
many in that day! Her heart was given to the
best of men; and untroubled by things that led
many weak women captive.

"I must write to my naughty, darling Bertram,"
Lady Adelaide said—questioning though, how she
could ensure his coming home.

When she had first written a short note to Mr.
Bowles, for the Earl, saying what day the wedding
was to be, she wrote and sent off to her pet boy
a letter, full of affection and advice. All that
his father and she asked, was that he would come
to them and show now that he did not forget his
home and those who loved him best in the world.
She folded this, uttering many anxious sighs;
and sent it off to the village—vexing herself to
find out how soon it could be in her darling's very
hands.

# CHAPTER X.

A SMART, sleek young waiter stood at the door of
the mess-house inhabited by Berty's Hussars—
blinking his eyes at the sun on the gravel, and
flicking a napkin in his hand.   It was quite early
—not more than eleven o'clock.   To-day there
was nothing to be done, and nobody was astir as
yet, except an officer, apparently on duty—for one
saw him, through the open window of the ante
room, fast asleep on the sofa, a cigar still in his
mouth, and his uniform cap on.   Here and there
a servant or a soldier with a book or a blue paper,
crossed the parade ground.   And then came the
wary old corporal, who brought the morning
letters.   He greeted the waiter at the door, and
began to empty his bag.

   "Mornin', post-boy," said he of the napkin,

who enjoyed a reputation for wit. "Why don't ye give a double knock, as y' ought to?"

"I'll knock you, my chappy," answered the Corporal, softly. "Got a pint of anything to drink inside, I wonder?"

"Yes; we've got an old mug with nothin' in it," said the other, in a friendly way. However, all this woke up the youth inside. And at the same moment, down came Berty, in boots and breeches, a red coat on, and hat at the back of his head. "Hulloa! Poor old boy! On duty?" said he to the victim in uniform.

"Of course; just my luck. About ten minutes in bed. How did you get on after I left?"

"Oh! I don't know.—Here, Bevan, get me some tea and toast.—Mrs. Freddy would sing the 'Groves of Blarney' till one got perfectly sick of it. Then we had shilling unlimited. And every-one was sober—so infernally cautious, we never had twenty pounds in the pool. I won, I think. I'll be fiendishly late." And he began stamping and whistling. "That sweet servant of mine! Not a sign of one's horse, of course."

"Oh! you'll find 'em in those big woods, quite happy, any time till three o'clock."

But before the outrage on breakfast which

Berty permitted himself was half finished, a couple of hacks were being led up and down in front of the window. Berty's was in charge of one of his stable-lads, and his own man was in attendance also—to see that he didn't forget where he was going, when he had to come back, and so forth. "Look, I say, what cigars are these? Where's my lights? Is that brown sherry there? You've dropped my sandwiches. Did I tell you to pipe-clay that thong or not?" said Berty, without stopping for an answer.

"Yes, sir."

"Look here! pack my things. I'm going to London. Screw that flask tight again. Take my things to the Station, mind. You forgot all my keys last time. No, 'twas in London I left 'em. Telegraph to Frederick, at Buffer's, to know where my keys are."

"Yes, sir. What train you go, sir?"

"Good Heavens! man; how do I know?"

"Yes, sir. Have you got leave, sir?"

"By George! it's well 1 remembered that. I'll be late. All your fault, Philips."

But at that moment, fortunately, the Colonel was seen coming towards him—in uniform, and indeed looking rather savage.

" I'd advise you not to go up to him in that
get up you're in, Chubby," said another youth,
mounting his own hack, and cantering off.

" Hadn't I better write, Philips, don't you
think?" said Berty. " Oh! here goes—never
mind."

" Please, sir," says he, stopping before the great
man, and making a funny little salute, " may I
have a week's leave from to-day?"—And he
began to laugh outright.

But the Colonel assumed an air of lofty bewilderment; in fact, he did not know what was
going to happen next. " Now I wonder who is
this young gentleman?" he asked, in a tone of
wonder; and then he shook his head with mock
solemnity. " Why, I was a subaltern for ten
years, sir, before I dared to ask my colonel
for a week's leave. I've no doubt he ' wants a
pass to see his cousin, wot have come down
from London.' Well, go along, if you must.
Come into barracks sober, mind."

Then Berty jumped on his horse.

" Please, sir, these letters for you," says
Philips.

" *Will* you not keep me?"—And he stuffed his
mother's, and a few more letters into his pocket

unopened. "I'm not going to London, but to
the ball at Shawick. Order a trap and a pair of
horses for me at ten," he called out.

It was now about half-past eleven o'clock, and
he had to catch the hounds, some six miles off.
It was a bright morning, as he cantered along,
and the wind hurried great white clouds across
the open sky, freshening the air after the storm
of the night before. He knew of a short cut or
two, and went top pace most of the way to the
place. Here, he found that the hounds had just
gone straight away from a big wood. So there
was nothing to do but pull up, lament his fate,
and light another cigar. As he stood up in his
stirrups, listening on the top of the blowy hill,
and cursing the sheep-bells that would tinkle
worryingly so close to him, a great fat fox, with
a leer on his face and a brush as big as a bolster,
pushed through the hedge, and cantered across the
road a few yards from where he stood. Berty
never said a word for twenty seconds or so. Then
opening his little mouth wide, he gave three or four
good holloas. Something would happen probably
after that; and in three minutes time up came
the leading hounds, running mute till they
jumped into the road. Here, they checked and

spread out with an eager whimper or two, close under his horse's girths.

"Oh! you angels!" says Berty, watching their noses twittering, his horse 'the while recovering its wind. Then, from a stifled whine, an old hound broke into a lovely note : *that* was the place, and no mistake! The rest swarmed eagerly to a gap in the hedge, and then away they streamed, gliding over the fields, like a strip of shadow on a windy day in spring.

Berty was tolerant of a gate as yet, and held the one out of the road open for the first comer.

"How 'do, Newmarch?" says the master, as they jostled through. "Not five minutes gone, you said—Eh?"

"He's just in front of you. We're in for a cracker, ain't we?" Berty answered.

"Ah! yes—'fraid there's three foxes before 'em, though."

And they both took hold of their horses. And had to go along, for the hounds were now only just visible, racing clean away from everything.

"There's our place, Gournay," says Berty, ever ready to give advice to anybody.

"It's a gate, ain't it?" answered the master, steadying his horse as they came close. But it was only rails, with the posts fixed in a peculiar way.

"What they call a gate in this country, is it?" muttered Berty.   "Hold up!" and he sent his little hack at the timber.   The rails ran close by the trunk of a great tree, and he had to lie back to save his head from the lowest bough; but they were both safe over, and then the grass was capital going.   The Master muttered something about the river.   By this time four or five more men were up.   " Where's the ford?" asked every one, as they came to the cold water rippling between the chalk banks.   No one to be seen save a couple of rustics in a punt, grinning and staring at them.   " Be a ford about a moile," the rustics said at last, very, very slowly, and repeated nothing but this to each hasty question.

" Ford in"—says Berty.   And drove his horse right into the water.

The little horse made a leap for it, and disappeared ears and all; then fought its way to the other side, and struggled, snorting, up the bank. Of course, Berty came out about a stone heavier in his wet things, and after that it was plough, and they had to go fast through it.   Luckily, the hounds checked in a wood a couple miles further

on.  " By Jove!  I'll make a hunter of this one,"
said Berty, jumping off.

" Sew up that cut first,  I would,"  remarked a
sporting doctor who knew him a little.  Then
Berty saw that his poor little pet had staked herself slightly.  " How's she bred,  Newmarch?"
asked his friend, patronisingly.  " By Jingo, out-
of-sorts,"  Berty answered, examining the cut.

And  now the hounds—casting themselves—
picked up the scent again out of the wood, and
most of the field all swung off the road and went
to work again.·  But before they had gone over
three fences,  Berty on his tired horse, sticking
close to a tiny whip on a great chesnut mare, got
from him a  lead over  some  new rails—went at
them too  fast, and  his  hack, catching them
with her knees, turned over—like a wheelbarrow
down a  hill  side—and crushed Berty under-
neath her.  It was a let off for the man who
had intended having the place next, anyhow,
as he jumped off on the safe side, and climb-
ing over,  picked Berty up insensible.  Two
or three men came back to help, and he was
laid on the grass, his great dark eyes half open
his face perfectly livid, and the mud and grass
clotted into his curly hair.  The fall had a very

ugly look at first.   But it was not all over with Berty Newmarch yet, and when he could sigh and swallow some brandy, he got on his feet again and looked about.   "Oh! yes, I'll take, 'miss'—no play," says he, staggering up to his horse.   "Thank you; where am I?   I'll do very well now."

He got into the saddle and set his horse going again.   But it was no use, she was completely beaten, and the hounds, too, had flashed clean out of sight by this time.

"Quite sure you don't want any more help?" says everyone, passing and leaving him alone; and by and bye he found himself stumbling along on a tired horse—he hadn't the least idea where.   He could see that it was a large park they were in, and the fox had gone close by the ugly brick house.   "Can you tell me whose place this is?" says he, to a farmer, who overtook him at last.   "Why, Squire Orby's, to be sure," says the man, and went on. It struck Berty he'd like some luncheon under the circumstances. "I must know the chap who lives here," he settled; "have a try, any how."

And wondering to himself which of his friends these people would turn out to be, he rang the hall door bell. After a long wait a footman came. "Mrs. Orby at home?" asked Berty, tapping his boots with his whip.

"Mrs. Orby's been dead, sir,—some months," the man answered, in a tone of awe.

"Of course, I forgot—Mr. Orby," said Berty.

"Yes, sir; what name?" and he led the way to a great cold drawing-room, and left Berty there.

"I wonder where the deuce I am," he reflected. He had an awful head ache, any how.

After some time the servant returned, and led him through cold passages to a room, where sat at luncheon a grave, white-haired man of about sixty, an ancient lady, and three pale girls, in mourning. They rose one after another, and bowed to little Berty, in his muddy red coat.

"I'm afraid I've made a mistake," said he, lisping with a more complex lisp than usual. "I thought I knew you all; but I had rather an ugly fall, and didn't know where I was exactly. My horse couldn't go on; 'thought I'd ask leave to put him up. You know I'm very sorry, sorry to be in your way."

Mr. Orby only gave a weary sigh and pointed to a seat. "We are very glad to see you, sir," he said.

The old lady begged him to take luncheon, as he must be faint; so he began to eat. The three girls offered him what there was. But not a word did anyone speak. At intervals the old lady smiled, and Mr. Orby sat with his eyes fixed on the table cloth.

" You had a fall?" said the old lady, at last.

" Yes, my horse turned right over on me, I believe; don't know where it happened. He was the smallest horse I've got."

The girls turned their heads, looked at each other, and all shuddered together.

Mr. Orby was not paying any attention. When the stranger had had enough to eat, every one rose. It was evident this was some one who had met with an accident, and there was always hospitality for a forlorn red coat in that out of the way country. " Your horse is not rested, sir," said the old lady.

And Berty made this out as a hint to stay. He followed them to a brighter room than the first; a blazing fire was in the grate, and the old lady sat herself close to it, and folding her hands, took little further notice of him. The walls were covered with pictures, and Berty stared about at them; then at the three sisters sitting in a row.

"We hope you were not hurt," said the three girls, together.

"Oh! no; I always fall light some how. But then the horse must be light too, by the way," he added; "he can't weigh much."

"Shall you be afraid after to-day?" asked the youngest sister.

"That would never do," laughed Berty. "I should tell you—I'm a soldier."

"Are you?" said she, examining him with curiosity.

"To be sure," cried Berty. "Why, here's a lot of horses," and he began eagerly examining a picture on the wall. "Are these yours, Miss— 'm 'm—?" He had forgotten their name utterly, so that wouldn't do again.

"Oh! no; they were papa's before we were born."

"D'you like horses?"

"I think hunting them is cruel. That picture is one of Millais' early ones. Do you like him?"

"Who was he?" asked Berty: and the girls, looking at each other, began to laugh. So Berty laughed also.

"It is Sir Raoul the Rebel."

"Oh! tell me about him," he begged.

"I will; do you never read?"—

And the eldest looked at him with gentle pity.

' (If I tell them I read ' Bell ' they won't know what that is '). "Not much," he explained. " I can't."—

Then they all laughed again.

"I mean I hav'n't much time; but I'll read about this when I go back, I promise. What a jolly view," he added; "I'd like to live here," and they all went to the window. " You're not going to tell me the story after all, I believe? Are you going to the ball at Shawick to-night?"

They shook their heads.

"Oh! of course not," says Berty, confused. "It will be very stupid—if you don't go, I mean."

They opened their eyes taking this in good faith.

" Can you do this puzzle?" said he, lifting one from the table.

"No; we've had it for years and can't find it out."

"Oh! I'll shew you." And they were not a little struck by his gifts of adroitness. Then he shewed them ever so many tricks with a handkerchief and a piece of string. After a while, even, he made the youngest hold her hand for him to experiment upon. " Now I'll twist this string in and out," he said, taking her innocent fingers in his. " There, you just do that, and you see it's gone."

After that, he and the girls sat at the window twisting cat's cradles; he perfectly happy and unconscious of where he was. They talked low, so as not to disturb the old lady ; now and then he laughed, and they stopped to listen to his laughter. " Shall we have tea by and bye?" says he. " I like tea at five, don't you ?"

" We have tea at eight; will you stay, do you think ?"

He shook his head.

" What's your name ? I've forgotten," he asked of the youngest, whom he had taken to specially.

" Oh ! ' Edith,' " she answered.

But that wasn't what he meant. Thus they talked till it grew dark. She told him about nearly all the books she read, and he determined to get them immediately. Suddenly, he remembered how far he had to go.

" I have paid a long visit," he said; " and trespassed on you, I'm afraid."

But they were very sad at wishing him good bye. The old lady had just woke up. He bid them a sad Good-Bye and gave the groom a sovereign at the door.

"By the way, what's your master's name?" asked he. "Orby; ah! yes. Turn to my left, and straight through Empney village, eh? Thanks." And he cantered away, deeply in love with the gentle being who had told him so many interesting things.

When he made his appearance at mess he was greeted with astonishment. "Here he is," says the general voice. "You've no business in society, sir; there's a funeral party warned for the purpose of burying Cornet Newmarch, to-morrow morning," and so on. But Berty shook his head sadly, and kept silence. "Well, why ain't you dead?" they enquired. "Bagenall swears he saw you break your neck over a post and rails—and met your ghost afterwards."

"What did you do with the fox?" asked Berty, in a subdued and saddened voice, having eyes for nothing but the champagne subsiding in his glass.

"Ate him handsome, after an hour and forty minutes."

"Ah! I went and had luncheon with an

Angel !" he said, pensively—(" I knew it; he's a ghost," observes some one)—"so divinely innocent, 'pon my word; got no mother! Do any of you scoffers know people called Orby ?"

" There he is again; nineteenth woman he's been in love with this week. Moment the hounds settle to their work, Mr. Chubby pulls up—and begins ruining the peace of all the motherless orphans in the neighbourhood."

" Yes; and on Sundays," says some one else, " I'm told the young ruffian goes about to all the churches in the town to see the servant girls. Friend of mine who knows those places told me about it."

" What a deal of good sermons that boy must have heard in his time," it was suggested; and thus they went on in a delicate vein of Military criticism, while Berty consoled himself with more champagne.

In a couple of hours he and his companions were pulling off their overcoats in the hall at Shawick. There was the gusty music of a waltz, And the lofty rooms were ablaze with light and gilding—and golden hair and flowers, and pearls and glossy shoulders.

As these persons of the cavalry persuasion

made their long wished for appearance, two young ladies, Miss Ethel and Miss Maud, stood looking for them. And when Berty sauntered up and lounged in the doorway, pulling down his sleeves like a count of romance:

"Here comes my little guardian angel," whispered the elder—Miss Ethel—a haughty, worn-looking girl, to her sister.

"Indeed, dear! when did he tell you so?" answered the other, or Maud. And she went off savagely to dance; while the elder, who remained, beckoned to Berty so sweetly, that he woke up and went and talked to her, and they danced the next four dances together.

"How pale you look," she said, as they sat on the top of some stairs, and he told her about his accident in the chase.

"I want to go to sleep," said he, simply. "Talk to me and tell me stories."

And accordingly he laid his head back wearily. "I say; why was Maud looking so savagely at me, I wonder?"

"How do I know, my Bertram?" Ethel answered, gazing down on his round waxen eyelids, for she was a sentimentalist, and cared for these things.

Then they talked in a desultory way. While the music sounded hollow and far away below. Ethel thought " there is a servant coming."

It is the part of the flagitious only, to watch the flirtations of the ball-room, and of the passages near it. Hence there will be no report possible, unless some one comes rustling up to this landing—as presently Miss Maud did. With the centurion or captain of Berty's troop. " Sweetest, how wise you are to come up here to get a breath of air," said she to her sister. " Why does that man make his rooms so chokingly hot, I wonder?"

The sisters were each perfectly well used to the other's custom—of separation from the world with great friends. Berty Newmarch, too, was a very old flirtation. Still, when Maud saw him idly playing with Ethel's bracelet, which he now wore, she gnashed her pretty teeth. For she wished Berty to make love to herself, instead of to her sister.

The other Hussar, who was older than Berty, said, " What do you want here, you young criminal? Go down and dance."

" No; I like this," Berty pleaded.

So they all remained. For Berty had long been on terms of intimacy with them.

Again Berty spoke.  " I say—a bald chap with a moustache came up to me half-a-dozen  times with a  long speech; kept  telling me, ' there'll be supper for all  my  friends' somewhere; hoped I'd ' enjoy myself.'   Now, who was he, Maud?"

" That was the master of the house, you child. He makes cotton dresses, you know."

" Never saw  such  a  ball  as this.   I like it, though.   I've been asleep,  haven't I  Ethel?   I had a fall over some rails, you know."

" Yes, my boy, of course you have slept."

" Am I pretty when  I'm  asleep ?"—" That's why you  forgot all  your  promises, I  suppose," interrupted sister Maud.

" What promises ?"—And here Berty  thought of a good many lying about.

" Somebody wrote and promised  to  dance  the first waltz and the first galop  with  somebody," Maud went on, seeing her elder  sister  gradually getting angry in her turn.

" Miss O's. driven it out of his head," said the other gentleman.

" Who's Miss O., sir?"—and Maud, stretching across her sister, pinched  Berty's  arm  till  he writhed.

" Oh !   Ethel,  keep  your  sister q uiet," he pleaded.   But the elder sister was too  furious to

interfere. "Who's Miss O.?" he went on.
"Well, I say, do you know a beautiful being
who lives in a brick house with brown eyes and
fuzzy brown hair and no colour and so divinely
innocent—like I was before I knew you.
Well—"

"That's Miss O., is it?" says Ethel.

"No, I mean Orby, really. Who are they?
tell me."

" Pooh! the Orbys of Shereside, I suppose.
Everyone says he killed his first wife, and has
been inconsolable ever since. The girls never go
outside the park walls. They're perfect
savages," Miss Ethel explained. "Let's go and
dance."

Afterwards Berty, meeting the mother of these
young ladies, begged her to allow him to conduct
her into supper. Not formally, as expressed here,
because she was a strange, talkative old lady, to
whom one said anything. Nevertheless, as the
out-of-the-way things that are said and done at a
ball are quite unlike the exact language of a book,
we will suppose him to have been very polite.
Berty took possession of a servant and made him
bring champagne. Now this was the third time
that this motherly lady had been in to supper, so

she said, " Extraordinary people ; very strange house for us to come to, Mr. Newmarch. A man no one had even heard of last year. I don't know why I came, I'm sure. My poor girls would bring me. My Maud, she likes you shocking young Cornets and Lieutenants. No good, I tell her; you've got no fortunes."

Berty earnestly denied this; but she continued—" Does my poor girls good to hear a little nonsense now and then though, I believe. Your poor dear aunt—Penelope Felton—Mr. Newmarch, used to hold up her hands at me ; said I was quite a heathen and a brand, you know. And poor dear Newbury—such a handsome young man then—he'd say ' don't scold Maria, sister; her heart's in the right place.' Capital supper, I tell them," and she shook her diamonds and went on eating.

" Have some champagne, won't you?" lisped Berty every two or three minutes, having absolutely no other conversation, and the confidences to him increased in proportion as he was attentive to this great lady.

Then up came Miss Maud, with her last partner, an ordinary man, an average well educated English gentleman, such as one meets; perhaps a barrister; perhaps a magistrate for the county. She was come to have supper, also; but seeing Berty, and her sister no longer with him, she turned to her partner. "No, I don't care for anything," said she. "Are you not going to dance with me, *caro mio?*"

This to Berty.

"Of course I am. Have some of this? Like Moselle better?"

And Miss Maud took some. Berty took some also.

"How cruel you are to-night," said Maud, as the music sounded hollow and far away below. "You have never even spoken to me, my boy. Would I have come here to-night—to this stupid ball, to these horrible people—but to meet my boy?" And she looked tenderly at him.

"Oh! I daresay! when you wouldn't even talk a word to me at the Huffbys—just because old Sir Francis Debytt was there.

"Ah! Bertram! unkind!" she murmured; "when I dream of you day and night. Are not my prayers, waking and sleeping, for you? *Mine* are; but *one* I know," says she, "never prays for you—*one* you preferred as a partner, to-night, to Maud."

"Let's come and sit higher up on these old stairs," he advised, when she paused for breath.

"You promised to come to the meet at our house, instead of hunting with the Southcliffe, on Tuesday. I pined for my Bertram, and where was he?"—Maud added, hurriedly,—"There is a servant coming, I know," or words to that effect.

He said, arching his eyes, perplexedly, "This is like the stairs I was on before. Now, how's that? Who gave you that thing round your neck? No, it's your sister that has got the Emerald one. I say, are you going to be in London this season? D'you know Mrs. St. Cyprian? She says Ethel paints,"—and so forth.

And they went back to the crowd, where the ordinary people were amusing themselves. Berty was a popular person. He was spoilt, and could do what he liked. As for Miss Maud and Miss Ethel, they were so rich, and such great people in the county, that they did not care. It was all many, many years ago.

Berty danced next with a married lady, really very plain, who, making for the shrouded billiard-room, asked him if he could value the friendship of a true woman. This made him melancholy.

" Have you had any supper ?" he asked, later on, meeting the mother of these two young ladies before-mentioned.

" Well," said she, " I think I will just go and look for my two girls in the supper room."

This was in truth but an excuse. So Berty took her in to supper; and when people were going, he found their carriage for his friends.

As he took Miss Maud down the steps, she whispered, " What a waltz that last one was, Caro !"

Bob Sackville stood at the steps of the carriage; Miss Maud, all a haze of soft wraps and cloaks, turned to shake hands; and Berty, putting out—his for one last fond pressure, encountered an affectionate squeeze from the strong fingers of Bob Sackville, for Miss Maud, wishing to be kind to both, had confused between these gentlemen at the last moment. Hence the two rough hands had gone astray. " Hullo, old boy !" said Berty, as the carriage drove off.

Bob Sackville smiled placidly.

" Now, sir," said Berty, to him, yawning; " I'd like to go to bed soon; haven't been much lately. I telegraphed for rooms at the hotel here, so you'd better stay there instead of going back to barracks with those other duffers."

As they stood, some half hour later, in the hotel passage, smoking a final cigar, faint voices were heard not far off. Berty put his finger to his lips. "Hulloa, here's some one I know," sad he; and opening the door of that room, walked in, causing some faint despair to the two sisters, who stood by the fire in beautiful silk dressing gowns, like girls in an engraving. "Come and live here, Bob," he said; "I told the people to put some brandy and soda in my room, and we'll give these some. I'll fetch it." which he did. And then the boy thoughtlessly sat himself down in an arm chair, and begged Miss Ethel to drink from his glass.

"I don't like it; it's not sweet enough, and you are a little wretch," said she, parting his beautiful curly hair with the tip of her glove. "And what are you doing here, sir, I'd like to know."

"I'm thinking of Miss O.," he answered, simply.

And, thereupon, Miss Ethel drew herself away with contempt.

"Do not mind her," said Maud. "Give me your glass, Bertram. I will like it." It, however, nearly choked her.

"Mayn't I part your hair if I like," Ethel whispered; while Bob Sackville stood calmly surveying the pair. "Make the little cub talk and amuse us," said he.

But before many seconds Berty was peacefully asleep in his chair; and Bob Sackville gravely finished his glass. Whereupon he had all the talking to himself.

No doubt it was all very novel. But entertaining two young ladies—who are very jealous of each other, and can't smoke, is rather hard work.

The gathering light of dawn began to break in through the window curtains, and Berty slept calmly in the arm chair.

"Look at the babe," said Ethel; "shall I wake him?"

"No, let him slumber," her sister replied, yawning. "I'm very tired; I suppose he is."

However, she shook Berty until he awoke.

"I'll read about Sir Raoul, I promise," he muttered, starting up.

"Will you now, you child?" Maud said, looking intently at him.

Bob Sackville was a thinker, also the kindest of beings, when you came to know him. He imagined they had had enough of this.

"I'll carry this youngster to bed," said he; and wishing them good-night, lifted Berty up like a hat box, and vanished, in charge of him.

"I say," Berty enquired of the 'boots' next morning, "any place one can telegraph here?" And he confided to the man in a very hazy fashion what he intended to do, giving him half a crown at the same time. For Bertram never felt on easy terms with this kind of people till there had been a money exchange between them—wholly disproportioned to his income on the one hand, and the service rendered on the other. After spoiling half a dozen sheets of paper, he made out a message to the head waiter at Buffer's. "Send my brougham to meet me at station at three fifteen." "I must telegraph to my servant, too," said he. And that done, he slept in the train to London at last.

"Who's here, I wonder?" thought Berty, tumbling out of his brougham into the passage at Buffer's, and running up against little Church-wardyne, at that hour just going out to buy a new hat. "I say, Frederick, ask the cook to give me a

lamb cutlet—not burnt—and put some of that in
ice." Then he took up a lot of letters lying about.
" Mr. Rufford's in Egypt; Mr. Sale's never been
here, I'll swear, Frederick—says no one can live
here who's once been to Strong's.  Sir Henry de
Bream's *en cruche*, as the French say, Frederick.
These can't be for me.  Why, they're bills.  I
say, Frederick."—

" Sir."

" My Jew been here ?"

" He's dead, sir."

" Why! there's Mr. Lyster's servant.  *He* can't
be here.  Which is his room ?"

And he pushed by three or four hang-dog looking men in earnest conversation with Mr. Lyster's
man ; kicked his door open, and found the occu-
pant sitting up in bed, one arm in rolls of white
linen and a sling—while an ancient chamber maid
fed him with brandy and soda from a long
tumbler.

" By George ! old boy," said Jack Lyster ; " I
was just going to make Jane finish this B. and
S.—thought you were my doctor.  Fancy, if I
had now. "

" How are you, Jane ?" says Berty.  " Why,
what's happened, old man ?"

"Happened! blank everything. Why, broke my arm riding that fiend ' Escurial' at Aylesbury —the charming animal bolted over the chains, pitched me into a Manchester List Firm's trap; broke my arm, as you see, and—if I hadn't lit with my head in the centre of Harry Levy's carcass, and he hadn't been a fat man—broken my neck. I say," he added, " did you see a lot of duns as you came in?"

" Well, I thought I saw Bob Meyer's nephew, and that young ruffian from Pond's. Didn't like 'em."

Then they had a council of war, and made things out to be looking exceedingly ugly for Jack, as far as human knowledge could discern. At last, however, it was discovered that he could get out, and he and Berty had a modest luncheon in the brandy and soda haunted coffee room down stairs.

" I say, Frederick," says Berty, " if I win the Grand Military this year, I'll make you a present of a carpet for this handsome floor of yours."

" 'Be the ruin of the house, sir."

" Is my trap coming with that new pair, Frederick? You know, Jack, I want to go down to old Jimcrack's. The barman at Bunny's—he told me there's a parrot there worth any money—

uses worse language than Charlie Bedford, I understand—and they don't want much money for it either. I've two new nags to try, and so I'll drive you down this minute, if you like."

"I should think they'll ask a pony for the bird if he can do all that," remarked Jack.

Half a dozen men strolled in by and bye, and of course Berty forgot all about the parrot and Jack Lyster, and drove somebody else behind the new pair down to the club, where they had a couple of glasses of sherry each, as it was now five o'clock. Here Berty found a card for some dance, and a note from his Aunt Ellis, asking him as a favour to go to it. "Who ever heard of these extraordinary people?" said he.

And as his friend had never heard of them either—they being respectable people of some property and influence—into the fire went the card. However, there were three or four other things to go to that night. May be that in those days, March was the height of the season—or people hunted and got falls, in June. Either.

Berty went back to Strong's, and he and some others posted themselves at the window there to mock at the passers-by.

"I've got an appointment in the city," said

he.   Some one said, " A fellah must go into the city to get hanged, because Newgate's there." "No," replied a second, "they can do it for you in the Borough now."   "That's in the city, tho'"—"Lay you a poney it isn't."   "I'll take your six to five about it," and so on.

Berty then slept till it was time to dress, and he finally dined with the man on guard at the Bank.   About twelve o'clock he went to an early party in Berkeley Square, or thereabouts.   He was not the least amused there, and found himself persuaded to sit on a cold staircase with Mrs. Saint Cyprian.

"You little heartless wretch," she was saying, bitterly, " you pretend to care for me.   And what is it you don't do ? You never answer my letters. You cut me in the street every day. And when I give you tea in Hill Street—you talk to my eldest daughter instead of to me.   Yet, yet," she said, gazing into his astonishingly beautiful eyes, " I could teach you how to love as you never dreamt of loving.   Provoking boy ! Didn't I teach you to spell ?   Do you remember how you used to spell *soirée* when you wrote me your first note—with a W and two R's, child ?"

Already but a year or two from home, and he had learnt so much.

" Now what on earth is a good thing to say to
her," thought Berty.    " I can't remember her
Christian name for the life of me.    What was it
that woman at Shawick said ?    Ah ! yes."—

" You offer me the friendship of a true woman,
I believe," he lisped.    " Will you choose me in
the Cotillon every time—what *is* her Christain
name?—and we will be friends again, won't we ?"

" I will this once, child.    Let me see, what
flower will you be ?   I shall be a gardenia."

" I think I'll be a cauliflower," warbled the
young reprobate, opening his perfect and silly
mouth to laugh.

There came a Cotillon in due course, wherein
many young ladies openly made a point of choosing
young Hallmarke, who had last been launched,
and was the best catch of that year.    The bells
rang, the looking-glass was veiled over, and the
little flags waved.    And the room full of most
charming and enviable people amused themselves.
There were numbers of ordinary and moderate
men and women who did nothing remarkable.
It was a very delightful little dance—everything
was so *soigné*, a Paper said next day.    That may
be ; but with Berty, who carried his mother's
letter about with him—and had tossed  it in his

pocket among the other coats and hats down stairs, we are alone concerned. He went and had supper, and Mrs. Saint Cyprian and the Cotillon were utterly forgotten. For he found a girl to dance with who had never been to a party before. They were more of an age, and they made great friends.

Then he went to Lady Haybill's, to which everybody adjourned later. It was an immense affair, and there was no one he cared to see except Tommy Plunginton, silent in the supper room, regarding a wonderful salad. He meant to eat it by and bye, he said.

Then these two chatted about people's looks, and how they danced. How badly So-and-so was painted, and so forth. After which they had some champagne.

"I've had enough of this place," said Sir Tommy, bitterly. He had by this time found the salad hollow, and a snare.

"So have I," said Berty. "I have been bothered somehow all to-night." Then he told Sir Tommy he'd give him a lift anywhere. "You know I feel very melancholy," said he.

"Ah! I know," the other said, sympathisingly. "I think—if one didn't respect age and all that

—some one ought to tell her she's a great deal
too bad. What a pretty woman she was, though,
a few seasons ago. Might be a Grandmamma
now, and," added he, " if they hadn't sent George
Ayntree to India, I dare say she would have been
by this."

" Well, I mean to say, I think it is hard on
one. How did you know I meant the same person, though, Tommy ?"

" Why," said Sir Thomas, gravely turning over
an empty decanter for the second time, " we
were just above you on that staircase."

" Ah ! to be sure; yes," said Berty, somewhat
awed.

" You know, I tell you, I don't think myself that
it's quite good enough," continued Sir Tommy;
" she looks shocking badly of mornings, I understand. I happened to be living at Brompton not
long ago, and coming home in the mornings, one
used to see her regularly, going to the Oratory,
about seven o'clock. Her complexion and all
that quite gone by daylight." They were now
in the entrance hall.

" Mr. Newmarch's braw-um stops the wa-a-ay !"
some cried out.

"Now," said Sir Tommy, "never mind giving that man money.   Yes; *you* can go away."

As directions to the japanned little coachman, he said one short word.   The brougham horse plunged discreetly in and out through the drift and eddy of carriages, working its way up north-wards, beyond the fashionable region where Lady Hayhill lived.

Berty and Sir Tommy were too well satisfied with themselves, and too dignified, to talk much. When they had gone up Regent Street, as far as the lower end of Langham Place, they turned off into a gloomy, ill-lighted street by the church, and here all was dark and silent for a while, until a turn brought them to a string of cabs "setting down" for another ball.   They were before an unlighted house, however.   Now and then, a narrow stream of light issued from a door and flashed upon muffled up figures scurrying across the wet pavement; then the light was in-visible again.   Some one, however, was at ' home ' near Portland Place.   They waited their turn, and then the brougham door was opened by a seedy link-man, who, however, knew them quite well, and had a word for Captain Newmarch, and a hope for the Epsom success of that great favourite who was 'identified with the interests' of Sir Tommy. So it was written at the time.

Then the door of the house was opened, and a little *mon-orchic* Jew grinned a welcome to them as sincere as that of Lady Haybill. But though that lady may have had some far-off motive of interest in being civil to a baronet or a young man of property, here—on the other hand, small profits and quick returns were the rule. They paid half-a-crown each, therefore.

" How do, Ikey," said Sir Tommy. " Full, eh ?"

" Full, Sir Thomas! Yes, Sir Thomas. Take your coats and 'ats, gentlemen. Captain Thoropin's 'ere, Sir Thomas—askin' for you. Half-a-crown heach, gentlemen," to two new comers.

There rose and fell the thrilling sounds of the Waltz of that season. It was like wine to Berty's young head. He was as light of heart as a school-boy on a May morning. The lamps and stairs, and everyone he met, seemed cut out to please, and all was one long laugh, till it was the utmost he could compass to keep up that vacant and *blasé* expression which—copying Sir Tommy—he knew he ought to assume. Fifty

acquaintances met him there and made him welcome.

Thus far, the letter which Lady Adelaide Newmarch had written to her eldest son, announcing
Helen's wedding, remained unread.  Not so that
one which she had sent to George, to St. Abbs.
For it lay, even at this very moment, before
George Newmarch, under his lamp's light, in his
college room.  He sat alone : it was near the
arrival of dawn, in the spring morning, and he
was dead tired, all alight with a kind of fever, his
feet deadly cold and his lips burning.  In the
last hours he had been going round all his
mind—seeking for some outlet whereby to escape
the weight of the sentence pronounced against him.
He was weary of saying "she is forgotten."
That was like beating against a high rock with his
fingers.  He could not keep hold of such a
belief as that, or rest thereon.  It would not
take the form of a truth.  And he knew truth,
when he saw it.  "Well, instead ;" he said,
"my wretched, disowned love is inside of my
heart, out of reach of rubbing away ; like the
black in an Indian's skin !"  It struck him how

deliriously he spoke. " A while ago I was beginning to believe I had forgotten her, and was glad. But see! here it returns. By and bye, I shall pray. When I fail utterly in reasoning, I shall pray—pray it away!" Afterwards he read several times, as follows—

—" and dearest George, we must all make a point of being there, since we all wish well to dearest cousin Helen, and must shew that our good wishes accompany her in the important step she is about to take. As the journey is expensive I send the enclosed."—

In his open desk he saw the crumpled Bank Note which his mother had sent. And there also were the dusty ends of some old Oxford bills. Midway, in his confusion of mind, he began to look these over. Vast sums—and he laughed at them. But it was a pitiful joke. These could never be paid. For he had no money. And so he left them alone and gradually floated his mind off to another life. When he was older and all this day by day drudgery —of rising, and being tired, and bearing misery—was abated for good and all, he would be happy. He would be ever a grave man—seldom smiling, loved by children; and loving best to talk to them. Where there were people sick and in pain, silent and not requiring rapid talk, there he would be best welcomed—where he would hear his own voice reading, and comforting.  It was not hard to picture such sights.  The sick man or woman with hands clasped outside the coverlid, and listening with bright eyes to words of Peace. After those works he would go home to his solitary room and kneel all night praying for Helen.  And for her children.

She would be grave, too, when she grew older, and would not care to talk much, and would have a sad look when he or any stranger met her.  She, sitting like this (for he beheld her plainly), working while her children played. Then he had a fit of shivering ; for he remembered, " Were not WE TWO"—(a potent phrase)—" once dear to each other, and no one had the right to forbid us ?"   George now breathed hard, his red eyes fixed on the empty wall of the room, his mouth drawn down.  There must be some way to solve this.  So he said, " I have had my death since the Island day.  1 am dead, and here is a new life—of peace !"  So rising, he went into his bedroom, and knelt to pray.  Such prayers ! his head constantly throbbing the while.  He prayed out loud. But a kind of conversation went on briskly all the time between Helen and his dead self—step for step; till the talking had the bed of it. Nevertheless, he remained for an hour, as he believed, on his knees, so that they became cramped, and without feeling. "I have been a long time. I shall kneel till daylight comes."— So he intended, but in a little while was so weary that he fell forward on his bed—and slept.

While he was thus employed, Berty was dancing at that place. There had been a fight. It was Frank Kerseytor, who insisted on coming in in his shirt sleeves. The door keeper refused to admit him, and in an instant Frank and his friends were pushing and struggling fiercely. Berty strove his utmost to force his way to their assistance, but before he could reach the battle place some one lent the intruder a coat, and there was peace. Then Berty asked Frank to be one of his supper party.

"Here, Newmarch," said Sir Tommy Plungington, seating himself among the glasses at Berty's table. "You come down to Drakeford with me and see Jim Pierce's lot tried. Frank

Kerseytor's coming, and there's something of mine going to be put through. Give one something to drink, some one. I've got a 'special' waiting at the station, and we'll be there in an hour. I telegraphed to have it come off, and Jim Pierce 'll have a trap to meet us at Drakeford Station."

"All right," said Berty, who would have agreed to any conceivable proposition at this moment. "Only just let one go down to Buffer's first. We'll all go down together. You'll go down, and you Telegraph to old Jim Pierce to have breakfast for us all. You see," he explained to some strangers who were standing about, "I give all my money to Frederick, at Buffer's, to keep for me. He gives me just enough for the day. The only father I've got now, I always say."

Frank Kerseytor got into his own clothes at Buffer's, at last. Berty put on, "what I call my 'private trial' suit!" for he explained, "one must have the correct suit for each sport." And half an hour later the three were sliding along, in a first class carriage, past the house tops, above the still hushed and empty streets at the Surrey side of the Thames; while behind them, towards

Whitechapel, the streaks of red before the dawn were just commencing to rip through the screen of cloud and fog.

Berty sang without ceasing. Frank Kerseytor abused him for making a row, and Sir Tommy smoked and read " Ruff's Guide." " I say, this thing's all wrong. Surely 'Diaper' didn't walk in with the crowd, in the Prendergast ?" said he. " I say, Frank ; what 'll you put on at Warwick, if this filly can do old 'Policy' at seven pounds ?"

" Two apes."

" I like you ! You know well you haven't got a pony on earth, you old humbug !"

" I don't care. Get you to back a bill for me. Hold your row, little boy ?" And then Frank shied the three cushions at Berty's head, and Sir Tommy began to read again. " You're nice duffers," said he, thoughtfully. " What do you know about anything ? How 'm I to tell what to back ? How am I to know ' Policy's' in form ?"

" Why not have him weighed !" says Frank. " Why, you ought to know. He ran something to a neck—at Lincoln, didn't he ? I know you let us all in, over it."

" That pig-headed Jim Pierce swears it was 'good enough line' "—mused the baronet, beginning to yawn at last. But then they slackened speed coming to Drakeford Station, and here a dog cart with Jim Pierce and one of his lads, was drawn up waiting for them. "Good mornin', Sir Thomas; good mornin', gentlemen," began the trainer, with what is called a friendly grin. " Knew you'd be in time, Sir Thomas. Anythin' new in town, Sir Thomas?"

But Sir Tommy was not going to talk like a finishing governess to anybody. " Jim Pierce, you blackguard; Jim Pierce, you scoundrel; Jim Pierce, you precious unfortunate idiot! What are you talking about? You etcetera, you blank etcetera! You allow me to back that brute 'King of Brentford,' last race at Nottingham, and lose a monkey straight off—you unmitigated duffer!" commenced his irritated employer. "By blank I'll never give you a farthing of money as long as I live again. I'll tell every-one what an idiot you are. By anything I told Sir Conduit Cockspur, yesterday, you were the greatest fool in England—wanted to send a horse here. I told him, might as well send a horse to the Bishop of London to get ' fit.' "

"Ah, Sir Thomas! always hard on a poor man," said the trainer, soothingly. " We know your way, Sir Thomas—always full of fun. The filly lookin' *so* nice, too. Pon my word, Sir Thomas, I don't know that we haven't got a pretty good horse."

" Well, you careless ruffian, can we see 'em go at once ? It's gettin' late."

" Yes, Sir Thomas ; I think we can make room for all these gentlemen, if the boy walks."

The dog-cart rattled away briskly down the road from the station ; past little stucco villas, where the lodgers had not yet drawn up their blinds, and where rosy-armed housemaids turned round from their duties, with pail and brush before the door step, to look at them. Mr. Pierce, however, avoided the main streets of the town, and was soon spinning along the level chalk road, cresting the hill which overhangs Drakeford. As the fresh breeze from off the downs caught their faces and the raw mist began to lift away, to their right seven or eight horses came in view, following each other in sober single file, while, wide of the lot, sauntered a long, lean, black horse, in a yellow quarter-piece, swishing his tail and turning his head from side to side.

" There go the beauties !" cried Berty. " They

look as solemn as a lot of old ghosts. Why's that one going along by himself?"

"*That's* old Policy," said Sir Tommy. "He might take it into his head to savage any one of 'em if he wasn't kept a hundred yards away. And he looks well," the owner mused. "What's that weed going third, Jim ?"

"Oh, it's only a two-year-old thing of Mr. Crockby's. Nervous colt, sir; can't get any muscle on him"—

"Who'll you put on the old horse ?"

"That boy that's on him 'll ride, Sir Thomas. As good a man as there is in England, only he's a bit heavy. Ah! Mr. Kerseytor, he's been with me for years, and I never see Sam Evans get the better of him, for riding, in a trial yet. Married man too, Sir Thomas; got a family. Most silent lad you ever see, gentlemen. Put Drury up on the filly, I suppose, Sir Thomas ?"

"By Jove! we'll have that silent man in to sing songs till the train goes!" interrupted Frank. "I say, Jim, where are your touts? I expected to see your hills black with them."

"Lord bless you, sir; there's none about us. Leastways not till after the 'Craven.' There's 'Diaper,' Sir Thomas, going last."

" What a thundering brute she does look," observed Sir Tommy, from the very bottom of his heart.

" Well, what would you have, Sir Thomas. A light filly I always acknowledges, but look 'ow Providence treats her—chucked into every handicap Sir Thomas. Gets off wonderful smart too; wonderful!" Then nothing more was said, and on the top of the next hill, they pulled up and awaited the race horses. The morning was frosty and raw, and the stretch of grass looked sombre by the faint March daylight, while for miles around them all things lay completely hushed. " Bring the filly here," said Pierce, as the silent procession wound its way up. " Send the pair half a mile, I suppose, Sir Thomas; and the boys to do all they know?"

" Aye. They've weighed, I suppose," the baronet answered, shivering.

Pierce frowned and looked distrustfully at the boys. " Yes, yes, the old horse 'll carry about fourteen stone ten, and the filly eighteen seven. You shall have 'em both hexact when we get home, Sir Thomas. Here, boy !" he said, and the babe who was riding ' Diaper' jumped off, to give place to a hideous youth with an immense head and mouth. "See you get off level," cried Pierce, to the departing lads. "And you win just where I stand, at that fuz' bush, mind."

The silent boys nodded, and turning their horses away, followed the head-lad away, along the level ridge of sheep down, to where a bough stuck in the turf marked the half mile starting point. No one spoke, the trainer posted himself a few yards in front of the others and Sir Tommy's teeth chattered audibly.

"They're off!" called out Berty; and the two tiny shapes contracted, as the distant horses lowered their heads and settled down to race. "By gad ! how she slipped him," Pierce muttered to himself. They closed in together a little, and gradually grew larger—clawing away the space of grass that intervened with their nimble feet. "'Diaper's' race in a walk." shouted Berty, breaking the absorbing stillness. "No, she don't win." Frank Kersytor answered, clutching at some one's arm.

Pierce held up his hand rigid; and along the space of down, came through the hush of the morning, the thud of horses' hoofs smiting the earth. Then old Policy, sailing steadily towards the place fixed, slides his head up in line with the other.   And now the boy on the bay frees his right arm.   The white arc of his whip glittered against the grey offing, and fifty yards from them they heard the slash! slash! of twine and whalebone ringing on the filly's sides.   She did not swerve at all, and shot at once to the front as if she could come away from the old horse as she liked.   But Barret, thereupon looking in the other's face with a grim stare, squared his elbows and shook up Policy with a vengeance—who just stretched his wiry neck, cocked his beautiful black head on one side, and making an effort, passed the group—first, by a length.

Berty was sadly disappointed.   "Knew 'Diaper' was a brute," he said.   But Sir Tommy remained scratching his chin in deep thought, and Pierce rubbed his hands together, turned to his employer, and bowed to him with immense significance.

The two horses walked slowly back to them.

"I couldn't do him, sir," the boy said softly, jumping off 'Diaper's' back.

"You had to rouse your one, Barret? T'wasn't all your own way, eh?" asked the trainer, and the other gloomy lad nodded.   But a nod was quite sufficient for Pierce.   "That's all right.  Now, Sir Thomas, you can put as much as ever you like on—provided we keeps well. We've just got to tell the boy not to win too far at Warwick, that's all.  Mind, it's only 'cos you're particular I send the filly at all, Sir Thomas.  I call it a mortal sin to show up a 'oss that could"—And so on.

As they rattled back to Drakeford, Sir Tommy said, "First bit of real luck I ever had.  Jim, I'd have given that thing away a week ago, if any-body 'd have taken her off our hands."

"Well, Sir Tommy, it did come just as fortune do come.  I let her alone and she just took her own way and went on improving Providentially. And then see!  She comes out and runs a great fine 'oss like ours to a length at seven pounds."

Mrs. Pierce was laying out the breakfast things as they opened the door of the trainer's bright and tidy cottage, and she curtseyed very nicely.  "There's no train up before 9.45., gentle-men," said she.  "What'll Sir Thomas and the gentlemen take, James?"

"Nothing for me, Mrs. Pierce," said Sir Thomas.  "You won't mind, though, if I go to sleep on your sofa here for a minute?" and before many seconds, he was slumbering quite soundly.

"Now Mr. Kerseytor, I've seen you eat before to-day," says Jim. "Never off your feed, I might say. And you won't refuse what we've got, sir," he enquired, turning to Berty.

"Have you got any brandy?"

Mrs. Pierce poured him out a small glass. And taking the cayenne pepper from the cruet stand, Berty sprinkled the surface of the brandy freely with pepper corns and drank the mixture off without a word.

"That'll set me up for the day," he said.

"I like that now," Frank observed. "No swagger about it. You've got a Coroner here, I think you said, Mr. Pierce. Bet you a new hat you don't swallow the glass as well, booby." And then he sat down and ate everything within his reach, chatting away the whole time, while Berty played with a couple of kittens on the floor. Before long, Pierce had to leave them, to meet his horses coming home.

"That yours, Mrs. Pierce?" asked Frank, as a chubby little girl scampered into the room, holding up to view the corner of a torn frock.

"P'ease ma," she said, and then stopped, staring at them all.

"Wants me to mend for her, I'll be bound, Mr. Kerseytor. Oh! you naughty child," the mother said, bustling about. "Never has a decent stitch, gentlemen. And poor Mr. Levy promised her a new silk frock to nothing, if 'Slogan' won the Hearl Spencer's plate—and the 'oss goes and hactually gets left at the post, Mr. Kerseytor!"

"Eh!" says Sir Tommy, jumping up and rubbing his eyes. "Mrs. Pierce, you've got a pack of cards, haven't you? We'll have some blind hookey, till the train goes." And Mrs. Pierce lending them a very brown and aged pack, they sat in the cheerful, sunny parlour, and played away for the next hour. When they got up to leave, Berty had lost a few sovereigns to Sir Thomas, and received several of Frank's I.O.U.'s." "Mind, you're bound to be at Warwick, Newmarch," said Sir Tommy, in the railway carriage. "'Pon my word, I believe we've got the best thing I ever knew in m'life."

"Yes, I shall go back and get a week's extension, certainly," said Berty. "I suppose I can change carriages for our place, at Rufton Junction?"

"Well," Sir Thomas, remarked thoughtfully, "Jim Pearce is out-and-out the best cad I ever came across." And his two friends agreed with him there.

"I know several good cads," Berty observed. "There's my servant, now. He's a good man. You know I'm rather a Liberal. I like the lower classes and all that—if they'd only wash. It stops conversation so, when they don't. By Jove! doing squadron leader on a very hot field day! Did either you fellows ever kiss a housemaid, on a fine summer's day, when she was walking along in a great hurry, I mean—running upstairs, or that sort of thing?"

"I've kissed these maids, and never found them in a hurry at all," said Frank, who spoke to obtain renown.

"I didn't ask you," said Berty, scornfully.

"By Jove! you fellows see Charley Tylton's sister? What a pretty girl that is," said Sir Tommy, pensively. "I never saw her before last night, at old Lady Hayhill's."

"Why, she was at Melton all last season," Berty answered. "Stayed with the Brooksbys. Used to go like a bird, too."

"She's so desperately thin," urged Frank.

" So they say about you, I'm told, old boy."

" I think she's awfully ethereal and all  that," Frank continued.  " But I swear I had a good view of the  last race  for  the Stamford  Cup through her left shoulder-blade.  Well, bother! You fellows never will  believe a word I say; perhaps 'twas her shawl.  Why, look here.  I was dancing with her  at Mrs. Ffrench Graye's lawn business this year—and she stopped to drink a cup of tea in the middle of  the waltz, you know, and by George! when I put my arm round her waist again, I could  distinctly feel  the tea descending among her poor little ribs."

Sir Tommy yawned.  " See you on Friday, then, Newmarch?" he said, as they parted at Rufton Junction, Berty just hitting off the eight o'clock train from London there.  In less than an hour, from the windows of the carriage, he caught sight of the  roofs of his own barracks as  the train ran into the station.  Stepping on to the platform, he did feel, for a moment, jaded and cross.  Yet, in those days  of youth and rich health, nothing was a  match for his high spirits.

The next thing to be done, he settled, was telegraph  to Strong's, and order  a wild fowl and a bottle of champagne to be ready when he got up to town. "I'll dress there, and have a quiet weed with anybody that's up. I wonder if any fellow here 'll go in for a special with one." Now since we first saw him this time, Berty had not had a quiet anything, anywhere.

While he stood on the platform, thus debating, he found that the patient Phillips was saluting him. "These letters for you, sir," said he, "and four telegrams. And the h'adjutan' been inquiring for you, sir—and Mr. H'eveley, he took your court martial, sir—and a hawse came down from Curry's—William said I was to mention—and that party brought the two badgers you ordered, sir. Beg pard'n, sir, a young lady's been come since this morning, early; said you had agreed to see her; give a good deal of trouble—at least, we feared she might, sir."

"Will you hold your tongue? How am I to get through all these?"—and he began opening some letters. "Where's a letter from Sawtry, that came the day before yesterday?"

"Beg pard'n, sir, you desired me to put it along with some more, in the pocket of that h'overcoat you've got on your harm, sir."

"Young lady, did you say? Is that her, there?"

And cramming his hat on the back of his head—which with Berty was the symptom of being in a fix—he tore open a couple of telegrams. They confused him; he let one drop and away it fluttered on to the sleepers.

—"There do pick that up, for goodness sake; it's from my commissioner," said Berty. "Take my coats—and this case, and give me a light. Find me that letter of my mother's,"—Which Phillips did, and lighting his cigar to help him to think, Berty read,

"Sawtry Marshal, Saturday.

"My Beloved Bertram—"

He frowned. And looking up, saw a young girl, like a governess, walking to and fro.

"I wonder who it is," he mused. "Must be some one I know. Are there any more, Phillips?"

"No, sir. Only that respectable young person in the hat, sir. Came yesterday afternoon, sir, and goes right up; mistakes the Barrack Master's quarters for yours, sir; wouldn't be gainsaid at first, and Mrs. Stalker, she went on hawful about it, and was for complaining straight to the colonel. I see it was a mistake, sir, took the young lady and showed her the Cathedral, and the principal objects of h'intrest in the town, sir, and conducted her to the top of the Castle Hill, and procured her some refreshment. A most proper spoken young person, and very well educated, I thought, sir."

"Why, it's Mary Slowly, from Sawtry," said Berty, surprised. "What the deuce does she want here? and how am I to get up to town? and how am I to get leave, and see after these telegrams? Here's Bob Sloman insists on another name. And then my account's three hundred overdrawn."

And as he thought the present a good time to finish his mother's letter, which had lain unopened in his pocket since Monday morning, he read it through to the end.

It was a beautiful letter, such as most lost sons have received while on the way. Meshes were woven across Berty's heart, but through these it gave little sundry sharp stabs. He walked about biting his pretty cherry lips, and frowning. It was because every one was bothering him. Everything went against him. Why were things coming in the way, and making him vex his mamma?—so he called her still, when speaking to himself. She hoped he was good and happy. He was neither. They would all bully and vex him here, and he thought they were a lot of brutes.

He was to come home at once, the letter said; Helen was to be married on Thursday. Who was Helen? Yes to be sure. And this was Wednesday. Probably—at least Monday had occurred some time ago; was the day he looked at the pictures with the little Orby girl, and had a cropper at those rails. He must start for home that minute.

Then he observed the girl who was waiting. "Oh! ah!" said he, going up to her with a questioning manner.

She began to cry.

"Oh! mustn't do that," said Berty, arching his eyebrows and looking frightened.

She continued to cry. There was the old policeman, who took the tickets, watching him out of one eye; the last flyman from the Black Swan also, leant over the paling, attentive and ironical.

Berty looked at the girl. She was undoubtedly Mary Slowly, whose mother lived by the lodge

gates at Sawtry. Berty had been wont to talk
to her in the evenings, when he had been at home
last—and walked about to smoke his cigar after
dinner. But he was perfectly guiltless here.
Had it not been so, perhaps he would have felt
less taken aback and alarmed. "You know if I
can do anything for you, I shall be very happy."—

She was as pale as death. He saw that her
shoes were worn out, and that her dress was
muddy, and that she could hardly stand. Meantime she had done nothing but hold a wretched
little handkerchief to her eyes. Nevertheless
Berty remembered that he had once given her a
twopenny brooch and several kisses; so he was
alarmed. "What train did you come by?" he
said, in despair.

"Come away from that man," sobbed she,
looking up towards Phillips and the porter.

"Hadn't you better go back to Sawtry?" said
he.

"You won't send me away. Oh! don't, don't"
she muttered. He wished himself at stables on
the hottest day in July,—on duty of a Sunday
afternoon—on the longest of District Court
Martials ; anywhere—well out of this.—"I
walked," she sobbed.

', All the way?" said he.  "Good Heavens!
when?  My dear Mary, you must be half dead.
'Pon my word!  Look here, if you'll go with
Phillips—and he'll show you a good sort of hotel,
respectable place, you know.  I'll come, and you
tell me all about it.  Do, for Heaven's sake, or I
don't know what'll happen.  Why, you'll faint;
walking five hundred miles in one day."—Without looking at her, he turned back to Phillips.

"Look here, Phillips," he went on, hurriedly;
"Now you're a clever fellow.  Look here.  Get
this wretched idiot of a child to go home, you
know; to Sawtry, you know.  Give her five
pounds, and pay her fare, and see she isn't
bothered.  I'll telegraph from Strong's.  I'm
going home for a week, and you must get a pass
and follow, and tell William to bring that new
bay horse—and the one I got from Lord Kill-
bally—by train to Sawtry, and start to-morrow.
D'you understand?"

"Yes, sir; and shall I pay the man for those
badgers, sir? because one's lost all its teeth, I
suspect, sir; and a constable's been about some
rats he says you let loose in the Independent
chapel with Mr. Heveley, on Sunday; been mentioned in the town, sir—"

"All right.   Look here!—I'll telegraph."

And Berty rushed up to the barracks to get more leave.  A hundred fresh things demanded his attention, till, Mary Slowly utterly forgotten, he was in the train, and speeding towards London, out of harm's way.   Then he suddenly jumped up off the cushion of the carriage, and stretching out of the window, he looked back towards the pretty valley and the foggy town, as though he could return there.

"Fancy the wretched child walking five hundred miles—isn't it ?   Fancy !"—

Then of a sudden he remembered his mother's letter.   He took it out and read it again; and then shut and opened the carriage window restlessly, and smoked away.   Like as the smoke of his cigar curled up, and was blown wide, and thinner, and thinner in the beautiful frosty air— so diminished the impressions which this wistful letter gave him.

When Berty descended from his hansom at the door of Strong's Hotel, it was nearly two o'clock.   Freddy Dopplevay (now abroad) stood, in his usual pensive attitude, thinking—with a tooth-pick ; gazing up the ascent of the street opposite.   Berty nodded to him, and going in, asked of the waiter,—" Sir George Ingarsby came back, Theodore ?" (or James or William ?) " He's in town, I know."

" He is stopping here, and he went out early. But I'm not quite easy about him, Mr. Newmarch. I feel 'little alarmed, sir."—

" How's that ?" Berty asked.   They had taken some rooms there together, and the fact was that no man's memory could stretch back to the last settlement of the bill.

—" Well, first, he's been sleeping here for four nights, Mr. Newmarch, and—"

" Looks bad, that, indeed," said Berty, hurrying off much relieved.   And then he went up to the joint sitting-room in question.   A number of men were at breakfast there.   And Berty had not the slightest idea who they might be.   They were fellows one remembered seeing about.   There were all sorts of things to drink—as well as breakfast.   Most of the fellows were smoking. They looked good sort of chaps.   " I suppose you came to see George Ingarsby ?" he said.

Some said, " Yes ;" but, indeed, they had each dropped in on the faith of finding nobody there, and thinking it as well to order breakfast, as there was no one else to eat it.   It was rather absurd of the man himself to come back, when he was supposed to be out of town. " Well, you know, I ordered a duck, I think," Berty said, and he rang. Somehow, nobody ate much, except one good-tempered sort of man. He ate away Berty and he talked about racing in France and Abroad. In the details of this he seemed thoroughly at home. Indeed, his mission to this country had been to make a prominent foreign favourite for the Liverpool safe, and success had waited on his efforts. He talked like fun, any-how, Berty thought.

Next, in came Bob Hanwell—(since quite out of it. In those days, however, he used to buy everything). He slunk up to the fire-place with his hands in his pockets, and his hat at the back of his head. He knew all the men, so it was all right ; but he didn't take much notice. Berty, who could never remain long with any one with-out relating all his affairs, laid the case of his extraordinary visitor at the railway station before Bob. It rather bored Bob Hanwell. " I never go in for that sort of thing," he said. " Come down to old Jimcrack's, and see some boa constrictors he's got for me. I'm goin' to turn 'em loose in my park, you know. Just had to blow up those alligators you saw down there with some gunpowder inside a bait, an' a galvanic battery. Ate all my canvass-back ducks, and a lot of water-spaniels and clean shirts of mine and some babies of my keeper's they said put 'em out to dry, and they ate 'em I mean shirts. wasn't it absurd you get yours from Eale and Binman, don't you? old Jimcrack—he said, 'Never heard they liked shirts.'"

Then the collector relapsed into gloomy silence once more.

"Come down and look over what Napthali's got," said Berty. "He had some grey diamonds last week that you ought to get, Bob."

But at that moment a telegram arrived for Mr. Newmarch—

"Got men here and a private steamer. Mean fight come off on quiet. Be at Paul's wharf two forty-five."—

That was appealing to Berty's weak spot, indeed. "I can get to Sawtry by the night mail, after all," he arranged, and set off instantly to be in time for this fight.

# CHAPTER XI.

WHILE Bertram Newmarch and his Corinthian friends are enjoying themselves in some tranquil nook among the Essex marshes, let us return to Sawtry, where all the wreaths and veils have been decided upon, and at the last moment come down in charge of a young person from London ; and where all the company are now assembled for Helen's marriage.   We shall hear much about her doubts and troubles, hopes and fears, by and bye.   At this time she walked, as it were, in a trance.   Lawyers had come down from London— greyish faced men, like doctors, or some kinds of tradesmen—but she had not distinguished them. There had been an assembly in the dining-room, and to her deaf ears the customary little legal jokes had been made ; everybody was in good spirits, and then, on the broad, black walnut wood dining table, the settlements had been duly signed and attested. And very grand they read. Their purport had been explained in due course to Helen, although her only desire, she said, was that these things should be left to far wiser heads than hers. Yet she had wandered back from her dreamland for a moment, once or twice to become aware of the amount; and then in her little simple way had known that, should Mr. Tresham die, she would be wildly, absurdly rich—for a child like her. But as this wealth and money was so far off—and had so many written deeds, and hard men about it, it did not seem real. Could she not, it had come into her head, be a widow first, just for a while; but that was only a fanciful half-thought which never matured itself.

Miss Helen had only a trifle of her own—hardly enough to buy gloves with. Lady Adelaide was to persuade Mr. Newmarch to give her her *trousseau* even. But was she not a rare treasure in herself. And Charles Tresham had so thoughtfully managed, that Helen's lack of fortune and the symptoms thereof, were entirely kept out of sight in making the various arrangements.

Lucy and Catherine Felton and two of the little Basledons, mere children, from Monksylver, were the only bridesmaids; while Mr. Curry, waiving his own convictions perhaps, was to marry them. It was to be entirely a family party, on the day. And to make it complete, came a person whom no one there had seen for twenty years—in fact, Lord Newbury himself. There had arrived a few lines from Mr. Bowles to say his lordship wished much to be at Miss Mallorie's wedding, but fixing no time. On the Wednesday afternoon, his own carriage brought him from Daryngworth to Sawtry. It was many years since any of his relations had seen Lord Newbury, and but few people knew what sort of man to expect. His coming, of course, would bring much honour to the wedding, and it was a comfort to Julia Tresham to be able to mention this guest, when she wrote about the event. Helen, too, began to feel that she had never quite done herself justice all these years—since so great a man had always been ready to take an interest in her. Lady Adelaide, though, could not be very glad. How many thick cobwebs, long grown over the past and its stories, this meeting brushed away! Indeed, that all their surprises came at once, was very hard, and those days did indeed try her. Save Stephen, everybody seemed to be pushed out of the usual groove ; the squire certainly was more savage than ordinary.  Little Helen was too shy and inexperienced to manage anything, and Mr. Tresham, who stayed at the rectory for the last few days, found himself, when he would gladly have been with Helen in quiet, somehow in everybody's way.

Lord Newbury was much changed since he had ceased to show himself to the world.  He was a strange looking man.  While most people brought but one valet when they came to Sawtry, Lord Newbury had two with him.  And one of these, a tall and grave man, who did not make friends much with the other servants, was hardly ever for a moment away from the Earl.  Thus, by the evening, all the relations were met together ; for even George arrived from St. Abbs in the afternoon.

Helen was just running across the gallery with a lovely bouquet in her hand, when he and she met.  She, for the first time that day, was not thinking of old times at all, and did not expect him one bit.  What had she to say therefore ?— " Oh ! George ! such an age since we've seen each other," said she, stopping short and out of breath.

It may be that he had looked forward to something less common place. He managed to smile. But before he could decide on a speech, she said, "Don't think me rude, but Lucy 'll never finish dressing if I don't take her her bouquet," and smiling, she hurried away. Then at dinner time half a dozen people engrossed her attention of course.

As everyone was going off to sleep, Mr. Bertram Newmarch drove up to the door. So could anything more be wanting to the symmetry of the family group?

The sun was out in glory on the wedding morning. Before this there had been a few muggy days of fog; then a bitter east wind; next it had frozen hard, and next had rained again, ending up with snow. But that fair morning George, who had lain awake a good deal, rose early, sauntered down the avenue, went out of the lodge gate, and stood still in the high road, leaning his elbows on the parapet of the bridge which spanned the head of the lake there. Staring at the cream of little weeds upon the surface of the water below, he thought what an insignificant thing he himself was. Circumstances had turned out quite right, of course. She was always meant to be great in some way—and what was he to her?  He had no money whatever, and no one cared to talk to him.  Why, he kept feeling in his waistcoat pocket now and then, and doubting if that miserable couple of sovereigns, his all, would even last to take him back second class to St. Abbs.  It was too small a sum to be even worth putting in his purse.  Let it lie where it was, in company with a knife, some coppers, and a key.  He had a poor shabby past to recall. He could not keep awake while he prayed even. The dawn has come, and found him asleep in his room instead of on his knees that day he heard of it.  And then, if he could be working his way to any fame! had he only been left a little longer at dear old Oxford!  To wait for years and years, where he was now— working without wages for his toil; while other people, whose lives had touched him, owned fame and youth at the same time—held the flowers in their hand, and still enjoyed them blooming on the tree.  It was fate, beyond his arbitrament, and he tugged at the oar in vain.  To enjoy the little sensual present was the paltry resource left to him.  Happy people could live for higher, nobler ideas.  He was too needy; yet generous youth revolts from the thought of giving up all angelic things and contentedly raking the mud for happiness. Better hopes remained. He had begun—it was not much, but was a start—to pay off his Oxford debts. How the self denial of that braced and cheered him. "Is there not," said he, "a delicate gratification in doing honourable things, outlasting the action, and remaining always by one, whence it takes a drain of self approval and contentment, at times of worry and dejection." He could "suffer and be strong" as he had read of. While chewing that fancy, he heard wheezing and groaning behind him; it was one of the old women in the village whom George knew quite well. The old thing stopped on the bridge and plumped down her bundle of sticks, being too feeble to carry them farther—coughing and mumbling to herself as she rested. She wore a tattered blue cloak, such as it pleased his mother to see each of her old villagers in. It was an idea of Lady Adelaide's to have them alike, all the winter; but she used to forget the fancy at times, and the cloak was of four or five years ago.

"Let me carry your load, Mrs. Humper," said George, hardly thinking where he was. She indeed could not see him, but knew what he meant. As soon as she could go on again, therefore, he shouldered the bundle of sticks, which was pretty heavy, and walked in front of the old woman up the road to her cottage.

"Am I going too fast for you?" said he, absently. But she was praying and wheezing to herself. When he got to the cottage door he put her bundle down and opened the latch. "Take care you don't stumble over them," he said.

"Oh! bless you, my dear," the old woman muttered, departing, and dimly seeing his face, "but's you be a little like mylady. I'd say you were her son. It's the inward fever's racking my bones this day, my dear!" and she hobbled in.

When George turned round there, close behind him, stood Berty, in the middle of the road. He was smoking a long cigar, arching his eyebrows, and inspecting his brother's movements with gentle curiosity. But George forgot to be ashamed. It was a year almost since they had met, and he could only think how wonderfully handsome Berty had grown. Drill and art had developed his brother into the most brilliant young dandy that George had ever dreamt of.

As for Berty, he thought old George, with his sticks and his old woman, simply cracked, or perhaps there was a pretty girl living in there. Might be either. "Do you do much of that sort of thing, old boy?" he said, thinking of Mary Slowly.

George blushed. "I'm awfully glad you've come, Berty. Of course you can stay for a bit? Isn't this wedding a wonderful event. You've seen Helen, I suppose?"

"I saw my father and mamma. I wish to goodness, Bo, they'd get another butler here. That brute Simmonds was three quarters of an hour getting one some hock and seltzer. I don't know what they're all at, I'm sure. But they bully you, don't they, poor old man?" What was all this wedding to him? What ever happened, Sawtry must be his in due time, and just then he had other things to think of. As they walked back down the road, George modestly asked how he liked his Regiment and a soldier's life. But perhaps Berty didn't want to be teased with questions, and they'd have talk enough by and bye. The sun going up over the farm sickened him. It had no pity. George would have liked to stay away from the house, where the clocks, too, went without mercy. Each time one looked, twenty-five minutes had gone.

"Of course you're all in raptures about this match," said Berty, "and her going to—Where is it he lives?"

George answered nothing.

—"Conceited little brute, she's grown, Tiff tells me; and no manners, of course."

"Has she?" said George, doubting now of everything. Perhaps she had, and if she were conceited and common, what in the wide world was real, and what to be believed? Berty surely ought to know. He met everybody and knew all the best people—with manners. What were the better people like? Would he ever see the divine ones, who made Helen common-place? He snatched at the minutes, which nevertheless, would not wait for him to settle questions. Then the very time came, and about twelve o'clock Mr. Tresham and Helen went into the church and were married.

The sun, descending through the lofty East window, traced a halo of light about the people's hair as they stood before the altar rails. The bride's costume was of white glacé silk, richly trimmed with Brussels lace. She wore a cope of white watered silk, fastened with gold and silver tassels, on which gold and silver flowers were tastefully embroidered. A brilliant diamond cross hung round the neck, the prescriptive orange wreath adorned the fair head, and a point veil dependant from it covered the whole of her person.

Then he ought to have been happy. It was related in the Daryngworth paper that—" The company having returned to the hall, a superb *déjeuner* was served in the dining-room, an imposing apartment, decorated with old portraits in oak frames hung round the walls. On this occasion, a tasteful bride-cake, ornamented with appropriate Scripture mottoes, was placed on a stand in the centre .of the table. "After doing ample justice to the *recherché*, viands set before the company, the health of the bride and bridegroom was proposed in an appropriate speech by Mr. Newmarch. The Rev. Charles Tresham, in a feeling manner, returned thanks. The host and hostess, and finally the bridesmaids, having been similarly honoured, the party rose and retired."

George's room was among the garrets under the roof. They were very good big rooms, but if you look out of the window there, you only see the balustrade which runs  rounds the house, and the tops of the distant trees.   However, by opening the sash and listening with all his might, he caught the sound  of the carriage and four, which was to take his Helen away, driving up to the door.

Then there was a  horribly long  delay, a faint cheer ascended from below, and the wheels rasped away down the avenue, bearing the happy couple on their journey.   He shut the window tight.

# CHAPTER XII.

The house was all quiet again when George walked downstairs. He avoided the library and drawing-room, where the company was gathered still; and, hearing Berty's voice in the dining-room, went in there.

A couple of footmen, with their coats off, were clearing away the flowers and silver, and Berty and Stephen stood chatting to the butler in a most amiable humour. "Come and have some sherry, old boy," said Berty; "you look as wretched as if they'd taken you and married you yourself. I say, Simmonds, haven't you any soda water up here? What Neologians the people are here, to be sure."

"I say, let's go on the lake out of these women's way," says Stephen.

"Now, my dear fellow, d'you expect that I

could pull two strokes?" Berty said, taking a great mouthful of wedding cake. "I'll have a weed, though, and look at you sculling, if you like. Don't smoke, eh? You'll have one, Bo?"

"I used to smoke at Oxford," said George, taking a cigar. He was thinking indeed, how the price of a pound or two of these would keep him in pocket money for six months.

The three went down to the lake the best of friends. The moment the boat-house door was opened, George's eyes fixed up on that sacred boat which had borne them on their enchanted trip last summer. What a dear friend it looked! Did no fairy shape hover about it? None, for mortal's eyes, while it, truly, stood in sore need of painting. Mrs. Tresham was at the station and in the train by this. But there are some things one cannot go on thinking about. Only he felt very humble and uncertain. He was glad Berty did not choose that boat. Tiff took the sculls and pulled them well up the lake.

"Let's get on an island," Berty said. "This old barge rocks so. It gives one D. T."

"That's your island," said Stephen to him. "You remember the poplar that's blown down; capital place to sit and smoke your weed."

" Ah! my island; I daresay."

A little landing stage had been specially built there, and three or four strokes brought them to it.   And here the three brothers sat on the trunk of the poplar tree in the sun, and talked over the events of the morning.

" Uncle Newbury's rather quaint; don't you think so, Berty?" said Stephen.  "He did nothing but smile to himself all through the breakfast and speeches and jawing."

" Yes, and you know I couldn't get him to say a word to me, either.   The people say he's rather like you about the mug, George.   You ought to have asked him what he thought would win the Derby."

Stephen laughed.

" I hate racing," said George.   " I know nothing about it, and I hate it.   I'm very stupid, no doubt; but I never saw many nice fellows who liked it."

" I say," Berty went on, " weren't you fellows frightened when the guv'nor began his speech? He generally says something awful.   I didn't know what was coming next.   She looked rather pretty.   What do you fellows think?   I'd rather like to marry her myself."

George heard that with pride. So he was not so very wrong in what he thought of her after all. It was a triumph to him. But he himself had not once seen how she looked that day. It was better not to think. He had his cigar.

"I say, Berty," observed Stephen, who never stopped talking; "the maids in the house like that soldier servant you brought—rather. They get him to do all their work. I heard that lazy Anne Carroll and Martha, persuading him to carry all the water upstairs for the people's baths this morning."

"Poor beggar, he'd do the whole work of the house, if they'd let him—and read prayers in the morning, too. Weaned all our troop-sergeant-major's children, they say in the Regiment. But that's simply impossible, I should think."

So the brothers chatted away.

By and bye Berty began to yawn and flag a little. "Here, my weed's gone out," says he; "not a light in one's pocket!" And he pulled out, a lot of Frank Kerseytor's I.O.U's., a round tin check with a hole in it, a loose five pound note, and a 'watch setting' report. "I'd like a glass of sherry awfully. Let's go back to the house. They give such stunning big glasses of sherry at

Buffer's—hold about a pint.    Where's George
Musgrave, on Monday, Tiff?"

" Oh ! Westney toll-bar."

" I'll write to old Doubleday and tell him to
send over a couple of his best uns for you, Tiff,
The parson here won't go, I suppose."

" I must go back to St. Abbs, on Monday,
early," George said.

The younger brothers did not mind Bertram's
patronising them.    He was a greater personage,
and had seen more of the world, of course.  Besides,
he was so utterly good humoured and cheery.
And then, the life he was in reality leading need
not come out now.    " I say, we'll have a season
together next winter, Tiff, when you can come on
leave.    You'll be out of the blues, then, probably,
parson."

" Can one get leave often ?" said Tiff.    " How
jolly."    Berty thus planned for Stephen's future
the same charming  walk in life he had selected.
It was a rare prospect for the younger brother.

After that they went back to the house.    A
few minutes of his society had quite atoned with
his mother for Berty's forgetting to write letters,
and not coming oftener home.    She was only too
glad to suggest and invent excuses for him, set-

tling that her Bertram would punctually do everything he ought to do from this out.   He had had
so many drills and duties, one should remember.
I believe that nearly all through the marriage, and
breakfasting, and rejoicing, she was watching her
eldest boy, and thinking about him; and admiring
nothing else.

"Was he not looking well?" she asked, of Miss
Tresham.

"Who? Charles? no I thought him looking
fagged."

"I meant *my* boy," Lady Adelaide said—selfish
for a moment. "Do you know, Julia, when I am
in London I am always looking at the young men
in the park and the street to see if there is anyone
like my Bertram.   But I never can see *one* to
compare with him."

There was a quiet, subdued party at dinner
each evening after the excitement was done with.
Most of the visitors were to stay till Monday.
Saturday came, and no one had much that was new
to say.  Charles Ellis and Mr. East, the family lawyer, tried to keep the squire in good humour;
George and Tiff entertained their cousins; and
Berty sat between his mother and Miss Tresham;
indeed, he was always the object of attention.

Mr. Curry was at Lady Penelope's mercy, and she took the opportunity to put many things to him very faithfully—determined that he should hear her now, since he perhaps was to be master of the situation in church the following day.

"I am sorry Lord Newbury could not stay," said Henry Stacey, who was the other guest.

"Yes. It was an unusual fatigue for him," said Lady Adelaide, gravely.

"He cannot bear much excitement, perhaps," Miss Tresham suggested; and then there was a pause.

"He does not look greatly altered," Mr. Stacey went on, for something to say; but as no one could conscientiously pronounce on that, an awkward silence ensued.

Lucy Felton began to ask George about Eton and his accident at football long ago. She thought perhaps it would amuse him to talk about school days, for she fancied he was out of spirits. It roused him up to recall that time of hot-blooded triumphs: and when he said something about the pain of his accident, it brought the colour to Lucy's face. The squire looked at her. —"Now, can you tell me, Miss Lucy, whether blood comes from the heart?" he cried from his end of the table. But by way of answer she only got still redder.—"Mrs. Charles Tresham used to say it did. What'll Miss Lucy and Miss Catherine Felton have to eat?" he asked, begining to carve. "I see, you're looking at the boiled chickens. I can always tell what my friends are goin' to eat the moment the covers come off. The young ladies, they all make eyes at the boiled chickens; and the old gentlemen— like Charles Ellis, here—they all fix their great eyes on the darkest ragouts."

The squire believed that Charles Ellis hated to be thought old, hence this was a standing gibe of his. Meanwhile, Berty had not condescended to talk much.—"Take this champagne away," said he to the butler. "Did you ever hear of such a thing as putting wine in ice? . . . *frappé!* My dear Stacey, the man has been boiling it."

"Well, do you know, Berty," Henry Stacey began, seriously, "a very large wine importer was telling me the other day that you ought never to ice champagne in a cooler—always drop the ice, you know, into the—"

—"Do they give you boiled chickens to eat at your barracks, Master Berty?" called out the squire.

" I have seen them, in salads, on the drag, sir."

His father frowned, and there was silence for a minute or two.

" The Eveleys were so sorry that they could not be with us for dear Helen's wedding," said poor Lady Adelaide, to change the subject: " Winifred is not the least better. Ah! by the way, Bertram—do you know Cecil Eveley? Is he not in your regiment? What sort of young man has he grown up? Is he as nice as he promised to be ?"

" Yes, I know him—looks about fifteen," Berty replied; " joined us last winter, with three steeplechase horses, and his tutor's wife. Greatest fellow to buy the deal at Van John and hold the King at *Ecarté* that ever I met."

" Oh! pray, Bertram, be careful; or I shall be obliged to leave the table." Lady Adelaide gasped faintly, amid general astonishment: fortunately the squire was not listening.

" Dear me, Julia, his mother told me he was so talented—did she not?" continued the mother, after a time.

" Ah! wants application, then, I should say," Berty suggested. " The young beggar sat next

M 5

me at the Exam., I remember; they gave him a
skeleton map of England—to fill in the counties—
and he set to and divided it into all the hunts he
knew.   And drew a fox going away across the
whole of Scotland: said Punchestown was the
capital of Ireland—that's incorrect, I understand,
Stephen?   You're last from school."

"P-p-p-punchestown's in Thibet," said Stephen, stuttering as usual. "It's where Artaxerxes
defeated Lord Burgoyne."

"Dear me! what strange things they make
young men learn now-a-days," Miss Tresham
observed: "and I'm sure it has done your young
friend no good, for example, Bertram.   As the
beloved Apostle said, ' Much learning hath made
thee mad :' I fear it is so in Cecil Eveley's case."

"Well—of course it's very painful to me, when
he will hold these Kings," Berty explained; "but
we have to see everything in our profession, Miss
Tresham."

"Yes, Bertram; too true, indeed: but what
I always say to young men is—' Whatever you do
have nothing to do with sin, my dear.' "

"Gives a narrow margin, though," muttered
George; but as usual with his sayings, no one
paid any attention to him. As for Miss Tresham,.

she did not like him. He seemed morose. Now
Bertram had at one and manner that almost
made up for boyish wildness and scrapes.

Berty began to be quite domesticated at home.
Indeed he brought many of his Regimental cus-
toms with him. He had reviving drinks brought
to him by his servant before getting up, just
with the same regularity as if he were in his
quarters; Sir Tommy and his race horses had
quite faded from recollection, and he honestly
considered that he had settled down to a steady,
hum-drum sort of life.

On the Sunday he and Tiff were late for
church—in fact, breakfasted about the time it
was over—and, as the two sauntered into the
library, they met the ladies coming in through
the window opening to the garden, fresh from
morning service, rustling their silks, and wearing
that complacent yet abstracted air which ladies
acquire at devotion. Nor would these dogged
young ladies—still meditating on what they had
heard, say more than " good morning," and that
with a certain tinge of abhorrence in their
tone. Berty, as soon as he got into the room,
cast a look towards the bright garden, thinking
on a cigar. The peacocks began to call in the

sun, and it was dazzling enough to draw the blinds down. The trees and flower beds wore that Sunday look that places have, and there stood Tiff in his newest clothes, and such a stiff collar on! His best coat felt so tight—that it could not be a week day. Berty saw yesterday's "Times," which had just been brought from Daryngworth, lying cleanly folded on the table. Now, it was an observance at Sawtry to leave it on Sunday untouched—till the squire, who had arrived at that great age which is superior to days of the week, had read it in the afternoon. But Berty made a dive at the paper at once, chucked away the advertisement sheet, and went straight to the column where the second day's Warwick racing was. He looked down the list, and, with a bitter feeling, saw what he had lost by not being there: for Pierce had not predicted very wrongly, and he read :

THE PIMLICO PLATE (handicap) of 50 sovereigns, for three years olds and upwards; six furlongs.

Sir T. Plungington's b f Diaper by Defence—
    Luna, 3 yrs, 4st 12lb                 (F. Cole)   1
Mr. Hulk's b c Olympus, 5 yrs, 7st 7lb
                                          (Penley)   2

Mr. Oleclo's b c Justin Martyr, 3 yrs, 6st 10lb

(Long) 3

Mr. Lag's b m Italics, 6 yrs, 9st         (Hall) 0

Mr. Bonnet's ch c Lancashire Law, 3 yrs,

4st 7lb                         (Babbington) 0

Lord Basinghall's ch f Schedule, 3 yrs, 6st 8lb

(Wilmot) 0

Betting—13 to 4 on Diaper, 2 to 1 agst Olympus, 8 to 1 agst Italics, and 30 to 1 bar three.

"Heavens above! what a hot one!" said Berty, awe struck. And then he read ou:—"Justin Martyr, on the right, was first off and made the running to the turn for home, where Diaper rushed to the front, had her opponents in trouble at the distance, and, coming on with a clear lead in the centre of the course, notwithstanding Penley's tremendous effort on Olympus, landed the 'good thing' in a canter by a length," &c., &c.

Could anything possibly be more provoking than that. "No doubt, Tommy heaped the money on," thought Berty, "and I could just have paid those Jews off, and everything, if I had gone there—instead of losing my time here at a stupid wedding." It made the place of his birth perfectly odious to him after that. And then that same day, his father had a long and irritating conversation with him. He might swagger before the womenkind, but Mr. Newmarch would not be put off, and insisted on some explanations, and an understanding as to the future. To be sure, Berty was most ready with promises, and finally an air of repentance and frankness which he could still assume, procured him a truce. Still he wished himself out of the place twenty times that day. There was nothing to do. George was no fun at all. He went to church twice of course, and mooned about with Lucy and Catherine, each with some old hymn book or other, for the rest of the afternoon. Poor George, had, indeed, grave thoughts as he walked with the girls that day. He had began the good fight at his out of the way college already, and he was not to faint or fly at the first threatening of a difficulty. Since it was wrong now, he would not go and look at the island, or think of it, any more. And then was it manly to repine? Didn't people get over these boyish fancies wonderfully soon? He had raved of some love affairs between himself and Helen, just as he tolerated lots of other unreal things in his brain. Doubtless she thought as much about him now as she did about Neal the groom.

On Monday after breakfast he had to start, and probably could reckon on getting a lift as far as Daryngworth. No one cared much, perhaps, whether he went or stayed; so while Berty and Stephen were fastening on their hunting spurs in the hall, he made his way upstairs and packed his own things without being noticed. "Frederick," said he to a fine red cheeked young footman, "you won't mind bringing my portmanteau down from the blue room, will you?" Hearing some one whistling and laughing outside, he sauntered out. Berty was standing on the gravel smoking, and waiting till the horses came round. "Off to Oxford, old fellow?" said he. "Goodbye. Ah! no, that other place. Got anything to smoke, eh? Have one of these weeds; some Knaresborough recommended me."

George took the cigar, hardly knowing what he did. And he held it afterwards in his shut hand till he was miles and miles on his journey.

"I'm going with you, please Mr. East," said he, and sat in the old chaise with his head bent in thought, till the lawyer was ready to start.

Those college debts would never lift from his mind.

In a few days, Bertram went away, too, and then the house was truly deserted. He left with many promises to his father that he would begin to reform with the least possible delay. No one at home could help being impressed by his grand manners and distinguished ease. In the servant's eyes he was a model of munificence. Quite the young prince. Now of course, fame of that sort can never be attained by pinching and saving.

That same spring Stephen was gazetted into the Army also, and left to join his Regiment, wherever they were. His start in the world was not such an event as Berty's had been, two years before, and it is to be supposed that Stephen knew to a nicety when he left home how many sovereigns were in his purse—and how many sixpences too. His cool head and even temper were not likely to steer him far astray, and perhaps, he had received a warning from Berty's scrapes, by which he would take profit. Things did go very smoothly with him therefore, and he enjoyed himself after his sober fashion. Many gather the impression that these young warriors have nothing else to do but to be merry and admired. A holiday life it must be, for they seem to be always putting on bright new suits of clothes; ever with cigars in their mouths, and attended by knowing servants, who keep bringing them things in long tumblers to drink. While in effect they seem to have no daily toils or engagements. Nor, best of all, any care for specie or intercourse with it. Business they may indeed be seen transacting, but that only extends to the writing of informal cheques—always for an even sum. Little indeed is the Share-list, little the Bank Rate, little the price of corn or meat to them—folk free from care, to whom life must be one long pic-nic.

On the other hand, George at this time was at St. Abbs, plodding along on his not bright road. As to worldly wealth, his allowance was now reduced to the lowest ebb compatible with paying for meals. There was not, certainly, much to tempt him to extravagance here, but sometimes he was in a woefully out-of-elbows condition, it must be confessed. He tried to take it all cheerfully. Luxuries, he said, were anything but essential to him. His present life was but a season of maybe profitable hardship; and then h had a pleasanter certainty to look forward to.   If he could only wait, brighter times were in store for him.   His mind had been made up to self-denial, and when he felt he was down in the world, he could console himself, thinking that he was one of an ancient and long-descended family, although just then he never by any chance had a spare sovereign of his own.   And that if his rooms were dingy and his clothes worn out, there was at Sawtry, state and luxury enough, in which he felt he had some part.   In this shabby hermitage, at all events, the time must  be spent till he had gone through the necessary studies —divinity and such like—and, being twenty-three, should be ready to leave St. Abbs to be ordained.   He had done with love, and quietly buried it out of sight. At rare intervals he had found himself stopping to muse over what he called his story ; the brief, brief time, and the  wistfully-remembered after-noon on the sunny island with her who was his mother's friend, and now diligent correspondent. Those were fascinating memories.   Yet a baneful indulgence, and ruinous to a healthy frame of mind, he knew.   While there was so much work on one's hand to do, so many foes, in his own breast and abroad to, contend against, such a host of temptations to spar with, taxing all his science, he thought, and his watchfulness—those poisonous longings but debilitated him for the real strife. Besides, he was ever too proud to whine and sigh for what was beyond his reach, or even to confess that he cared very much for anything that he knew was unattainable.

George, in those days, was a great pedestrian. On his solitary strolls, sauntering along with his head bent down, he would look forward to the time when, tranquilly settled at Sawtry, he should have the little church to himself. In his peaceful moments he pictured what he would do with it, and how beautify and adorn the well loved spot. He would have his father's approval, without doubt, then; and there would be all that the living brought in to devote to such a sweet task. On his worthless self, solitary and satisfied with a crust, he would spend nothing. About fifty pounds a-year would keep him; but when he had money he would fill every window with stained glass—that German process was considered the best. Encaustic tiles were wanted in the chancel. And looking forward to the Lectern he should cause to be made, filled his mind with satisfaction. He saw in fancy the walls glittering with colour

and gilding, and an altar cloth, most splendid,
gleaming beneath that window—perhaps worked
by Mrs. Tresham's hands—for in such ambition
sure there was no evil.    He in fancy reached to
weekly early morning celebrations in this church
of his.    Would not a plain-song choir, too, be at-
tainable for every day, with a little earnest effort?
He picked out in his mind the very children in
the village that he would persuade to join—for
what is there that energy cannot turn to profit?
he thought.    Such would be his task.    How
much there was to do, and what a far stretching
field when once one looked across it!    And then
Sawtry was without doubt the place, for, often
questioning that—he had been tempted to volun-
teer to a life elsewhere to some swarming town,
where he might labour from dawn to dark.
Some murky northern hive, grim with furnace
smoke and Protestantism and Dissent ; to toil
there and forget lost people quite; to prove himself in the furnace of intense work ; perhaps
to die quickly and to die in harness, like some he
had known, early taken from us, their little birth-
right of strengh and talent cheerfully squandered
in the church's " forlorn hope," and all laid down
without a thought of claiming thanks or fame.

Those lofty self devotions, above advantage or interest, had a strange fascination for him, and such a way as that was before him, too, though in another place, perhaps. Up hill it seemed. His load he felt already, and the night was going to be dark. But George Newmarch was tired of the world, which they had said was pleasant, and yet which held out no charm for him now. To neglect and want of sympathy he had long been comrade, and should he not gladly court them from this out in the better cause, wherever his lot might be cast? Of Berty he would think often at this time, shuddering at the blind, heathen life which was his brother's. Berty's pleasures, and the kind of people he knew best, were mysterious and shocking to George. He would sometimes try to lift his mind from his own quiet fire-side to the ball rooms and race courses, wherein he heard the other delighted; and then it was all a puzzle to him. He would light his humble pipe and smoke softly. He smoked still—some of the best of men did. And then there were hours that he would be so impatient and unhappy—he could not help it.

# CHAPTER XIII.

AFTER two years Helen was much prettier. During that time she was greatly to be envied in her married life at Norton Constantine. The gardens there are very fine, and Helen learnt all about plants and flowers. This increased the scope of her mind. She had a baby, too. It was a girl; whereat Helen felt deeply hurt. That was her solitary grievance. Yet she could not help feeling envious of the boy babies which she saw here and there, and experienced, it may be, a certain sense of poverty in only having given to the world something as good as herself. 'Constance,' they had christened their first born. It was a very thoughtful baby from the first, and a great companion to its mother, who could gaze on it and talk to it for ever. And then, in its small presence no acting was called for, and no one had to 'behave.' She was never tired of looking at this her child, for whom she now would gladly have died. She declared prettily that this should be *her* child; the next might be Charles's. For him, somehow, a new feeling sprung up. No one told her so, but their baby seemed to have celebrated a second and yet closer marriage by its coming. Such is the beautiful law. It always pleased Helen to think she was loving her husband. Often the little querist persuaded herself that there was no question about this. "This is love, is it not, which I feel?" And again, she reasoned, probably, if the truth were known, no such thing existed in real life as the love talked of in books; or rather if people would tell the truth, they always meant the same sort of passion as that which she now felt. She had resolved to be contented with the substantial well being which was hers, instead of pining for a love such as story books related. Thus it was in these days; Helen only thought at all when she had leisure, and doubts, therefore, troubled her head but at rare intervals. That first summer when they first occupied Norton, and she found herself mistress of that beautiful place, her satisfaction was un-bounded. In place of knowing anxieties and dependant fears, she now found herself at the pinnacle of success and good fortune. By her gentleness and by her witching face, and by making every one fond of her, she had won all this, and the consciousness of success turned her head a little. When she could be quite alone she became a child again, in singing to herself and casting off all care. Though she could not drop those former submissive and obedient ways in a moment, yet, when all petty restraints were no more, she was like a bird newly escaped from its cage. All this while her respect for her husband was unbounded. She fostered it diligently. "This is what Lady Adelaide predicted," she thought; "and how wise and right she was."

So in his presence her gentle gravity and submissiveness continued to be worn at all times. The summer was just beginning, when they came first to live at Norton. All the lordship there was Mr. Tresham's property—since his brother's death. The whole village belonged to him. Before he succeeded to the property, the rectory, which used to stand close by, had been his home, and he indeed loved every rood of the place intensely. Norton village is on the pretty little river Wayfe, three or four miles from its mouth; and the Wayfe, of course, runs into the Channel. Where it joins the sea, the southern coast dents in with a gradual sweep; low red gravel cliffs run along the shore, topped with a fringe of studded trees. At the river's mouth is Leet village. From the river there is to be seen nought but a black-looking inn, half a dozen cabins, and a long white-washed coastguard station. One flag-staff points up into the sky, and a few fishing boats swing at moorings in the roads, and are hauled up along the shore. At low tide you see wide stretching slob and mud on the fore shore, through which the Wayfe winds out to the sea—a few white posts only pointing out its course.

As soon as one gets away from the coast, however, the river twists in and out among pretty scenes, shut in at either hand by thick growths of woodland. So still and lonely is it as you ascend to Norton Constantine, and so richly is the stream set in a clasp of sweetest forest scenery, that one cannot be indifferent to the rare charms of wood and water here. There is hardly any traffic across this part of the forest, and the first bridge over the Wayfe is at Norton, close by the Manor house. The stream runs very broad and shallow just under Mr. Tresham's garden lawn. It is, of course, the back of the house which looks that way. From the South the wind, come last off the Channel, blows over this sleepy place clear and fresh at times, and wandering gulls often pass by from their stormy fishing grounds. Many ducks and herons build in the reed beds along the forgotten stream, and they are almost the only living things to be seen. Inland for miles you find the forest. Low growths of larch, oak, and fir mostly, with here and there open spaces of heath and common land. It is a difficult place to get at at any time, and one would think Norton forgotten by the rest of the world.

All the picturesque, quaintly-built cottages about there belonged to Mr. Tresham. One of his new projects, to inaugurate the new life, perhaps, was the re-building of most of these. Helen was to go about and give her opinion where changes ought to be made.

Mr. Tresham's land steward, of course, had always been for pulling down tenements, and for getting the poor holders and squatters out of the parish. How much fever these ivy-covered cabins could hold, too, was wonderful. But now Mr. Tresham was going to have cottages, such as land-lords put up in the North. It was an old idea of his, and he got together a lot of pretty designs. Helen thought every plan lovely, and would insist on being more delighted with each one in turn. "Only I shall want to go and live in them myself, Charles," she used to say. Mr. Tresham, at times, was busy with these matters all day long, and then his wife would ride out, with only the old coachman attending her. At first, through the village, she used to walk her horse—each person she met curtesying respectfully. But once in the forest, all alone, on grass grown sandy roads, or among the long rides cut in the woods, she would dash away at full speed, leaving the old servant far behind—generally losing the poor man quite; who often spent hours of terror watching for her. Her hair might come down, or her collar fly loose—she did not care. Those solitary gallops were glorious for a while. She could be a perfect child again, and none but little birds had eyes to look at her, as she sped along the narrow avenues—dividing the lacework of shadow falling there. Rabbits and pheasants dashed across her path, and no other living things would she meet. She said to herself she was happy there. Something lacked by and bye, though. When the novelty of sunny forest rides had worn

off, she began to want some other change. No
one certainly intruded on his and her happiness.
When they did begin to receive, the neighbours
to call were few and far between. The Hardi-
canutes, at Farwell Lodge, were the nearest. They
consisted of the Honourable Jean Hardicanute,
a proud woman ; her daughter Enid, who was
a wonderfully well educated girl. They had a
son, but some one had left him a property elsewhere, and he did not live here. There was
Mr. Hardicanute as well. He was a clergyman
like Mr. Tresham ; but he did no duty now, and
was without a living.

Helen did not like them, for they were envious
of her. They believed, perhaps, that Miss Enid,
being the granddaughter and niece of a Scotch
peer, should have had Helen's place. They were
not at all well off.

Besides the Farwell people, there was General
Rumbold, a widower ; his daughter lived with
him, and he had a yacht. No one else for many
miles. Such as they were, these neighbours
called at Norton and made friends with the easy
and unobtrusive cordiality of the high born
classes  Then Helen went to their houses in
turn : and after that she would have days an l

days to herself. Once—some six months after her marriage—for fun, she asked, could she be taken to Switzerland? But there were many things to settle, and Mr. Tresham had had much wandering about himself. He pointed out to her that they could never be so happy as at home. Mr. Tresham had got up a cricket club in the village; he was very fond of the game, and he would field all day quite cheerily, standing out in the sun in his wide brimmed hat and clerical tie. No distance was too far for him to walk. Nor did he mind in the least sitting up all night, if he had writing to finish.

That summer he prepared an interesting paper on Drycote Abbey, the place whither the party of girls rode, with him, from Rushworth. He meant to read it at the next Archæological Society's gathering. He was always happy and working then. To Helen he was kindness itself. Nevertheless at times, still she whispered, ' It is like being with the squire. If her husband had been but a little silly !'

Thus there was yet something she longed for : she missed somebody to talk nonsense to her—some young romantic person, perhaps—who would make sonnets to her eyebrows. Mr.

Tresham never did that. It was not to be expected. And yet he indulged Helen in every way possible, till, from getting out of the habit of controlling self, she became spoilt and selfish. In fact, just because she wished it a little, they did actually run over to Paris, for December. And on their way back stayed in London a few days. And perhaps in these voyagings Helen found many things to wish for, the existence of which had been unknown to her before. Hitherto, tyrannical self-consciousness had made the young wife afraid to as much as ask for more cream to her tea. She readily got used to strange people, however, and having a peculiar absent manner which answered as well as self-possession, did not, after a while, so much dislike meeting people who would notice her, and seem to think her original.

If she appeared to take a fancy to anything in those days, it was given to her. And let us consider whether this' is not the most happy state that can be formulated or pictured. Helen, however, soon said, ' How dull things you wish for become when you have got them!' Then she had, furthermore, no play-fellows to shew them to.

When they saw Julia Tresham again in London,

on their way back from Paris that time, she was till unable to conquer her prejudice against the Norton trees. Mr. Tresham, wherever he was, longed to find his face turned homewards again. The second spring after their marriage accordingly, found them at Norton for good. Then it was that the baby appeared: and as has been said it did make Helen extremely happy, although it was guilty, so to speak, of being a girl. Nursing the child was serious business. At first Helen pretended to know more than any nurse, and procured and studied sundry books on the question which, with directions from Lady Adelaide, gave her the airs of a *connoisseur*. But soon the poor little lady finding difficulties she had not counted on, lost her head, and becoming utterly bankrupt in resources, gave in, and left the command in the hands of her servant, who indeed was a treasure.

Thus the summer passed away. Mr. Tresham did not care for visitors, he said; and no one could make them happier than they made each other. He was beginning to get lazy, and considered a day's journey anywhere a bore. Once, however, they were persuaded to go to a pic-nic at Shottisham Castle. It was given by a Mrs. Barre, who lived a great way from Norton: and as she had taken infinite trouble to try and persuade Helen to come, it could not be avoided.

The party was rather dull : there were many ladies and few gentlemen. Ever ready curates were there, and one or two pupils—reading with the Rector close by—came also. Besides, a couple of the military class appeared ; no doubt on leave.

'I suppose they would know Bertram Newmarch,' Helen thought.  But they pulled their whiskers, and hardly said anything, when they were introduced.  And Helen hardly said anything.  So they went away.  Mr. Tresham made salad—that was not bad fun ; there also was a noisy genial man, who made all the company laugh.  Then there was some archery and dancing ; and people strayed about the grounds.  And, having had luncheon, the chaperons all sat together, smiling placidly beneath their parasols.  And with them sat Helen.  There were not many gentlemen among the multitude, as has been said.  No doubt some of the young ladies were pretty, some not so pretty ; and with the prettier ones the young gentlemen available wandered about. · Helen followed one or two of these cases with somewhat wistful eyes as they glided, along a walk say—close together ; progressing slowly ;

parasols twittering, as some very touching thing would chance to be said. When Mrs. Barre had paid Helen a little attention, talked about Norton, and about her baby, and exhausted the usual civilities, Helen again watched the stray couples— with a sensation, it should have been, of patronising superiority. For she had now a right. Was she not a matron, and by this time legally in the higher place? Nevertheless, a vague kind of regret and longing fell upon her. How did all that taste? She wanted to hear the sound of those inestimable things which people, with smiles and blushes and glancing eyes, repeated to each other. To have this sound in her ears. She had forgotten it almost. No doubt it was all great nonsense. Well, poor things, how young they were! She was beyond that; in the perfected development to which these chrysali, at best, but tended. Nevertheless she sat there, alone out of the sun, with a humming repetition in her head of this tune—that she had abruptly ended all romance without ever having as much as opened the first delicious volumes at all!

Thus Helen mused, desiring romance. Let us observe her again. She was to look at most innocent and fragile. One would have said she had some grievance. Some wrong done to her; which she forgave by the plaintive smile upon her refined and gentle mouth. She was just then dissatisfied that no one, of her own way of thinking, had been born to sigh for her, and love her devotedly for ever; some one as young as herself—perhaps a little older—whom she could admire; and think about when her eyes were shut. It will be seen that it was from having so little to do, and so much wealth and indulgence lately that Helen had acquired these thoughts, and they, of course, only visited her in petulant and envious hours. Yet once posted to her brain, they left a shadowy entry there, even though other ideas came and scored them over subsequently.

While driving home, she felt for her husband's hand, and pressed it in both hers. He was the only lover she knew. Fortunately, he was good, which was a great and sure reliance for her. He was the only man she loved. He, when she shewed affection, as in pressing his hand, used to look at her with immense trust and reverence, thinking her superhuman. Yet she did not half know how sincerely he believed in her.

" Are you listening?" said Helen. For a while she continued to smooth the back of his hand with her hand, and the carriage progressed at sleepy pace by long hedges, and by the skirt of those forest plantations. "Charles, let us talk."

"Well, my own?" said he, looking indeed straight before him, yet with such devotion, as though in front of a beautiful picture.

She was never patient of a long silence. "What did you think of the whole thing?" she warbled. Then, after a while coming to what was in her mind, she added, "Did you see how Constance Brownlowe and that Captain Seraphin went on? I never saw such a case—it was too absurd. Wasn't it, Charles?"

But he had not even been aware that either of these persons were at the pic-nic at all.

# CHAPTER XIV.

At Christmas they were all to go to Sawtry, where Julia Tresham was already established for the summer. Lady Adelaide, in these days, did not fail to write often to her favourite Helen, sending her long letters of advice. Bertram, from her account, was a constant source of trouble to his father. He seemed to have got into the most ruinous company, and matters grew worse daily. What with all that, and certain legal troubles of late, the Squire's temper had failed sadly. He did not care to have George at Sawtry at all; and the poor boy, as might be expected, had no enjoyment in his home.

George had altered strangely, his mother fancied; nor did he now confide in her as he used to do. When he was not with the Ellis's, he went about to one or two good-natured friends, who

asked him to their houses.  Divinity studies were
over, and he was only waiting now to be twenty-
three, to get ordained.  Of course, he had fair prospects ; but the poor boy had got into debt again,
and had adopted strange opinions.  His mother
hardly knew what he would be fit for.  That ran
in her head.  She would regret to throw away a
fine living like Sawtry, which one of the family
had always held ; but his ideas had altered so,
and he possessed so little self-control, that she
doubted the wisdom of forcing him to take orders
against his wish.  What did Helen think?

Such were the trials and crosses mothers had
to bear.—And the letter was eight pages long ;
and Helen was surprised into a yawn.  Poor
George!  He was going once to do such great
things.  And now—he was running in debt, and
quarrelling with everyone again.  'I would not
care very much to live at Sawtry now,' she
thought, placidly.  'I wonder what George has
grown like.  He had a soft-coaxing voice when
he was a mere boy.'

Anyhow it was very pleasant to be here.

Helen glanced about the shady drawing-room,
and her eyes took in with tranquil satisfaction all
the pretty things that were hers.  The clear

mirrors, the white marble chimney-piece, the rich-coloured carpet, her grand piano of polished wood, her pretty gold and leather books, and all the tiny, glittering things of ivory, china, and brass. A corteous light, sifted between the laths of the Venetian shutters, gave a soft flush to the ceiling and walls, whereon bright fruits and flowers were sketched. Outside, the living birds chirped through the blinds to her: and Helen rose, slid the window back, and stepped on to the gravel. A puff of scented air came from the hay-fields across the river as she, shading her eyes from the sun, slowly stared around.

Her green lawn stretched to the river's bank, as smooth as a table, carefully mown and tended, and—near her house-windows—broken up into flaming beds of flowers. There was a clear view towards the river; but, right and left, thick shrubberies shut in the place. No one was looking upon her, save ancient rooks going and hovering and turning in the high elm trees. It was here one would have first come, seeking contented people.

As Helen turned round to break a bit of myrtle off from the rich creeper which garnished the house walls, she saw her husband standing close to her. "Read your long letter at last?" said he. "Won't you get burnt, standing out there with nothing on your head? What does Lady Adelaide say? My letter is from Julia."

He was standing just inside the window, on the mat, which is a little higher than the gravel path on which she stood. Turning round, Helen balanced herself on her little toes, and with the aid of her two hands, managed to give her husband a kiss. He laid his hand upon her shoulder; and thus they stood looking over the lawn.

Across the river some young calves had got before a deserted lamb, and leaped and butted at it in concert, returning to attack the solitary and woolly thing over and over again, each time jumping stiffly into the air in their ecstasy. Then came a little boy in a glittering white smock frock, toddling across the field to defeat these his opponents, with a long stick. A woman appeared, and stood on the knoll, under the shade of some elms. They heard the sound of her faint voice, calling to the child. After that all was still. It was so peaceful and drowsy there, that Helen and he forgot how time went.

Mr. Tresham had had a long letter from Sawtry, too.   Lady Adelaide, his sister wrote, was greatly to be pitied with her sons.   There was something very strange about the family management, every one must agree, however loth to say unkind things.   He, for his part, thought there were faults on both sides, and the eldest boy had done things that could not be overlooked.  Helen was not attending much.

"I have thought, though, of asking George Newmarch to come here for a little," he went on. "One doesn't want a visitor, perhaps, much; but Julia writes such accounts of the scenes there, and of the father's strange ideas and temper—one ought, I think, to put up with a little inconvenience. I felt an interest in the young fellow, Helen; I believe he could be influenced for good.   I might be able to help him in many ways, perhaps."—

She straightway remembered the afternoon of the pic-nic, at Shottisham.   Why?   For no reason.   Why, should there always be reasons?— "what do you say, dearest?"

"Haven't I answered?   How absent I am. Yes, to be sure.   Which?   George?   He's always in debt, isn't he, poor boy?"   A hundred years before he had taken her in a boat.   And she got no dinner after it. Meanwhile, she held her husband's hand, inclining her smooth and small head in thought.

She fancied she had perhaps treated George Newmarch cruelly and left him broken-hearted ever since—dying, like young gentlemen in fiction, for her all these lone years. There was none but circumstantial evidence of this. But in a secret drawer of her heart Helen had always kept one or two such fancies, which their whole life long had never known what light was like. Poor George! He would talk to her, anyhow, and tell her about his travels. She was in a very different position now.

George Newmarch was not in London then, but he came a few days after this, travelling from the house he had been staying at, by a cross country line of railway and then by the steamer. The coachman who was sent with the dog-cart from Norton to meet him, said it was twelve miles to the house.

"Half-past nine now," thought George; "I ought to breakfast here, by rights. But I suppose there'll be lunch at Norton. And a fast 'll do me good."

He was a little savage with the world just

then.    Hence it suited his humour to go through
a small privation.    Besides, in truth, he had very
few shillings; so he got into the dog-cart, instead
of ordering breakfast at the Tresham Arms, at
Trele.    But the coachman did not find him in a
talkative humour.    He at times hated dragging
out his ideas—for people who could tell him
nothing new.    Eight or nine miles of driving
brought them to the top of a hill, under which
lay Norton among the woods.    " Is that low white
house Mr. Tresham's?" he asked, straining his
eyes towards this very burial place.    " What
d'you call that river?    Any ducks there? any
trout? any snipe in winter ?"—

Whatever the man may have said in answer,
George, for his part, did well remember who was
the mistress thereof.    He thought he'd get down
at this point where he could see the house so well,
and walk the rest of the way.    " I can think
better," he reasoned.    So the visitor tramped
along for a mile or two on foot, and at the last
rise in the road, stopped to look.

" So that is their lovely home !"    The low
white house and little towers at either end just
peeped above the trees.    Beyond the chimneys,
unknown woods rippled away in stripes of soft

colour, till they joined the blue sea and the clouds. Among the shrubs he made out a white bit of the river, close under the lawn. There was the spire of the church. The chimneys smoked; a cart went over the bridge, and red and white cows were grazing in the fields. What lay before him aroused an old rebellious sensation of envy and then of failure. People who lived in grand places like that would have little fellowship with him. And, in a fit of mockery, he recollected: ' How civil I must be to her now ! My former playmate knows no shabby straits and troubles. She hath no duns.' Such were his conclusions; which presently he was ashamed of. Had he not a sovereign intellect and grasp of mind, that he would not exchange for all the estates in the kingdom ? '' I suppose she has become stouter. And somewhat selfish, like the rest. And what a weary joke life is ? Would we even as much as laugh at that same joke, did we not want to pay court to the maker of it, whom we would gladly toady ? Here I am—returning to talk small talk and enjoy change of air over the grave of my dead love. Love ! 'Pon my honour, I have vast stores of credulity. I used to say I had unlearnt that word, one Thursday long ago.''

Thus this *blasé* young thinker indulged his reckless humours. Sometimes he said it was worth while encouraging this cynical temper, just to satisfy himself how vile a man's heart could be, left to itself. He had ever a fancy for criticising, in the most impartial spirit, the workings of his own mind.

The place was very still as he stood at the hall door, and the bell tinkled shrilly through and through the house, which was a quiet dwelling place, and most truly knew not how much it held.

* * * * *

"Mr. Tresham is in the garden deep in pruning," Helen said; "he will be so glad to see you, George. What years it is, to be sure! You must have so much to tell us about college—and all your doings."

She had watched him as he came up the avenue, smiling to himself, and peering at everything in his old way, and now advanced gracefully to shake hands. Had she grown pretty? He could hardly tell. She carried grape scissors in her hand, and wore a wide straw hat and garden gloves; and when she led the way to the garden, her very walk was strange to George.

"I never knew this person," he thought, within himself.

Mr. Tresham's welcome was very kind. There were all sorts of enquiries about Sawtry, of course; and George forced himself to talk—a little absently—looking at and thinking of other things all the while.

Helen had fallen off sadly. She was no longer Helen. Had they said she was a pretty girl. Yet this was a most pleasant hostess; there could be no question about it. Mr. Tresham thought George ought to see the greenhouses, and the river, and all the wonders, without delay. As it was a crisis in the laying of a border, he apologised for giving his visitor over to Helen for a moment.

George and she went about together, he with a pleased smile for everything she shewed him. Indeed, each turn presented fresh proofs of tranquil happiness and success. The sarcastic humour in force during his walk towards the house had perished, and cowed and spiritless as he was after his troubles at college and at home, Helen's newly acquired self-possession and grace of manner awed him much. If she had been gentle and engaging long ago—she had now invented new ways of being sweet.   Mainly a fresh smile, for company, as benefitted a hostess.   She wore on her fingers ever so many beautiful rings—signs of her wealth. When she had spoken in a hurry, and when once or twice she had laughed, George had seemed to hear again the flowing of the water in their lake, and the woods hereabouts became Sawtry woods.

They did not know it, but when they came back, neither had spoken a dozen words.   She said—" This is a forcing house"—for instance.

" Yes."

" The river—" waving her hand, absently.

" Is it like that ?"—

All this time he had had no breakfast, poor lad.   Returned to the garden, Helen—bored as he could see—left the two men together.

" You look over-worked and out of spirits, young fellow," said Mr. Tresham, taking his arm.   " That was the luncheon bell, by the way, tho'; come along."

They were rather a sober party.   Helen said little.   She had put on something to orna-ment her hair.   It was unwarranted—unfair.   In the shaded dining-room she looked more lovely than before ; her eyes obtaining some peculiar expression from the diminished light there.

She indeed liked to have George Newmarch before her. She compared the two men's faces— as faces; *his* was the best, perhaps, as one said of pictures. How fortunate that it didn't matter with men as with women. He seemed careworn, poor stupid boy. Perhaps she had made him unhappy at one period.

George sat there and had only seen her once, when she sat down first. His eyes were on anything else about the room. He was now sorry he had ever come to this place—saying moodily, "I bore them, I can see." Yet he chatted on with dismal facility. "I think I'll have some more of *that*," said he, observing some beef with mock interest and attention. "But I must tell you, Mr. Tresham, I don't eat at this rate *every* day."

"I'm glad our air makes you hungry. There's lot's more where this came from."

"Yours is glorious air. But, by the way, I remember—this is the first thing I've eaten to-day—So it is."

Helen looked at him with open, compassionate eyes. "Dear me! You ought to have told us the moment you came," she murmured; and in pitying, she looked precisely as she used to look when a child.

"Didn't Henry Slater give you any breakfast at Troylham before you started, young fellow?"

"Well—one left so early; I wouldn't let 'em get breakfast at daybreak, you know."

"Fancy!" said Helen. "Was it not wrong to allow him to start, Charles, and run the risk of being starved? How weak it will make you."— And her face turned as red as roses.

"Oh! nonsense; don't think of it," stammered George. ('Oh! then,' thought he, in an instant, 'she would be sorry for me.') "Why, I've often walked fifty miles, and far more—before breakfast, in the Tyrol and places. I don't mind it one atom, Mrs. Tresham."

"Hope you provided for your guides' families after those walks you took 'em, George," said Mr. Tresham. "You should have breakfasted at that magnificent Hostelry, the Tresham Arms, at—" But he stopped, remembring that perhaps the lad had reasons for being economical.

But the young man was asking himself in all ways—why she should have cared? And his enquiring eyes met hers for an instant. That recognition, disturbing him with vague fears and expectations, left him mute and anxious. She, also, had studied his face, finding in it nothing but ab-

horrence and a shrinking back from her own
eyes. Yet she could not subdue in her mild
glances this meaning—'When I am by myself I
will think about you.'

Mr. Tresham was asking if he were really a
great walker, then? He must try George's mettle
here, and accordingly repeated the distances of
some of the best and prettiest walks in the neighbourhood. He appealed to his wife to correct
him. She knew nothing of distances, though.
Such and such a place was an hour's—or two
hours' ride; that was her standard of measure-
ment. During which interlude George had time
to take breath, and to prepare to pull his fancies
up sharp and short; the Tempter having come
so scorching close to him in presence of Helen.

He did not see his cousin again until dinner
time, when he was thoroughly master once more.
And Mrs. Tresham, recently from her maid's hands,
appeared smoothed and decked out of any remains
of pity for his hungry state. Before he had been
at Norton an hour—said he—he had very nearly
made himself as wretched as he did at home.
He knew that he fretted wherever he went, of late.
At College, unhappily, he had not maintained that
discipline of patience and self-help with which

he set out. There was really such a thing as Fate, he believed ; and luck. Wherefore else did things always go against him ? In his hours of bitterness and neglect, he used to say, with a rueful laugh, that the Personalty of the Tempter—and the people at Sawtry Marshal—were together too much for any one man to baffle, and once or twice had all but given up. He was in debt before leaving St. Abbs, and when the local tailor, or whoever it was, came to oppress him, he would contrast this one with the polished Oxford tradesmen. Such poles apart ! Yet bills had to be paid, just the same coin was current, and demanded—up there, he found. By degrees, too, he had got into additional trouble, because utterly indifferent as to how his affairs went. No one asked him to decide on anything at Norton. There were no responsibilities ; no struggles and failures and jars there. It was a soft, unexacting life, and he was well content. There were plenty of books in the library, and he soon got into the habit of spending the morning on the lawn with three or four open beside him. Thus he got to forget how dull he had lately been, and how oppressed.

Mrs. Tresham had some duties to attend to, it

may be supposed. Hence in the forenoon George used to lie all alone on the grass reading; but she might now and then come to the open drawing-room windows and stand looking over the lawn. He would then lose his place, perhaps, and begin thinking.

In the cool of the afternoon, Mr. Tresham generally proposed a walk through the woods by the river. George disliked a set walk. He used to upbraid himself too, for being so silent—following Mr. and Mrs. Tresham along the pretty narrow path cut in the bushes, his head bent down, often in dread of treading on her dress, and saying nothing. How tired they must be of him! He knew he ought to be agreeable. And yet he could only make conversation for himself. That never stopped. He talked voicelessly to her nearly all the time. Yet she was the hardest to talk aloud to. He discovered that she was very shy. When he said whimsical things, she used, however, to laugh in her mild fashion, and so he got into the way of inventing little silly speeches for her amusement. Yet at times she hardly spoke at all. Perhaps she had not seen enough of the world—unlike ladies who went everywhere and met different people at every hour of the day, and who could whip round and get off like a shot, on any topic conceivable. But more probably she disliked him—did not wish him to be with her. This notion made the time very dull.

As time went on, however, they grew better friends. Before a week he had quite banished all recollection of her round brown eyes, filling with tears because he was hungry, the first day. That was just one of his old rebellious fancies. A compound of insolence and ignorance, which humbled him, and made him curse himself. He knew the worth of them, thank goodness! If she did dislike him now, it would only serve him right.

Indeed, when he thought of his own faults and follies, he confessed himself unworthy of such a woman's friendship. As he came to know her, Mrs. Tresham seemed more graceful and attractive daily. He said to himself that he had found at last an embodiment of ideal English Womanhood and English perfection, in its rarest form. Such a friend, gentle, thoughtful, pure, might fitly be his Guiding Star. To her his loyalty was due next to his Church in this world. And it made a man better to have such an one to look up to. And yet with it all she liked to be amused. It pleased her to be made to laugh, and they never got on badly, he confessed, when he was talking nonsense. 'Twas easy to fall in with that, too, for, said he, " it is not well to be ever serious."

Helen had a *naïve* sense of humour, and a childish fashion of criticising their old friends at Rushworth and Sawtry, which led George into the same tone. Their mutual shyness wore off as time went on. And then, one way and another, most days were spent talking over the books which he would get from the Library shelves— and about which he had many new things to tell her, things she would have feared to ask Charles, who was so wise—and rowing on the river together—he had been in Lower Boats at School, she knew. And all this, providing nothing else was to be done.

George must have read a good deal then, and there was hardly a title-page in the library that he had not mastered. Mr. Tresham had, uninterrupted, long talks with him. And other things happened. Yet, he learnt most from Mrs Tresham, he came to think; practical lessons that he truly much needed. Hence he gave her the largest share of his attention.

' How much more rational,' he said, often,

'is a common sense intercourse, such as ours—both reasonable, average mortals—than the boy and girl sighs and raptures that some expect. Aye! and pretend to believe in!'

He had not been so contented and cheerful for years. The Wayfe was a charming river to row on; in some spots full of weeds, but who could ever become tired of the view of green woods on either side there. So light of heart was he wont to be in these days, that he used to jump out of bed as soon as the sun was up, and go out, in the still and warm summer mornings, for a bathe and a pull by himself: till he, by degrees, came to know the river very well. He lit, too, on odd, dreamy spots, where no one ever came, except wild ducks and wood pigeons. 'He was giving his brain a rest?' he said. 'There was nothing to be decided just now.' Then, when he remembered to get back to the house, he sometimes met the lady of the place on the lawn.

"What did you see, Mr. Newmarch," she would ask.

"I saw some herons and pigeons. And some frogs—with large brown eyes, Mrs. Tresham."

Such speeches, in his quaint manner, made her laugh.

After a while he was privileged, when the evenings were cool, to take her in the boat down the river. He was sure that she was a thoughtful and indeed an intellectual person; and yet they never had much to say—of a serious kind—on those occasions. It was his fault, probably. And so, lacking anything better, they used to agree to tell each other what their thoughts were at the moment; every single thought. Then one or the other would recall something from the days when they were little at Sawtry. The bitter morning when she was sent to Rushworth, she had now blotted from his memory. And then, a few choking hours when he and Berty were together last, and she was married.—Well, they were over now. And how kind and pleasant it had all made her. 'We cannot always exact strict measure of happiness from the events of life,' thought George; and so, on the whole, though life at Norton was quiet and humdrum enough, he made the best of things, and was very happy. Often he used to forget what day of the week it was—hearing nothing all day but her prattle, having no occupation save the telling her some new thing; and she, laughing, would, when he asked her, confess she didn't know either.

They each had their favourite spots on the river to go to—his and hers—turn about. Now and then, darkness came on before they could get home. Helen would say, perhaps, " How often there are moons, George. Will there be one every night, from this out?"

George feared not. This, indeed, was a pity, for one bright evening they had remained long on the water, remarking how it was quite light. The Wayfe was most peaceful then. As they paddled idly along, the sculls scattered little shining drops of water over the dark water, which for a moment became diamonds; or as good as.

Helen's dress shone ghostly white in the stern of the boat. Her face was deeply shaded by the rim of her straw hat. " I can see your eyes as plain as day," George had almost said. But they floated along, and neither spoke a word.

The hour was one for continued thought. When fancies borrow a weird and singular colouring from the light and the place where one is. Sitting by the end of the boat, facing George, was something perfect; most lovely, pure, and fragile—a rare event shed upon the earth ; if, indeed, it had anything in common with the earth at all. This lady and her sweetness was the one subject whereon he reverently thought morning and evening now, with boundless awe and wonder. Was she not faultless? Such people at times were sent down to live amongst us—broken off, for our teaching, from another world, where none want guiding, and where there is, perhaps, a happy plethora of people like Helen.

A sense of her perfection kept him silent. And under this summer sky, on this their silent path hemmed with jewels, he only heard the waters welling off the bow. And the plash of his own thoughts; ever the same—always of her.

Helen remembered that it was night time, and lonely there. How kind he was! what trouble he took to please her! and he was so patient—although an odd and wilful boy at times. She pitied him. No one guided him; might she not? By this light he looked like a spirit watching over her. So she said. What eyes he had! Eyes owning a sad expression always. Like what? Did lovers ever look like that? Lovers—whereof they wrote and sang. It was late; and the lawn and house were far away behind them. 'Charles will be angry, and what on earth shall I tell him?' thought this traveller of the night. " Please row back quick, George," was the very first thing said by either of them.  How could she account to her husband for staying out in the dew.  It was fatally late, and as they drew in under the landing steps, there he stood in the moonlight.

While her guest steadied the boat for Helen to step on shore, she trembled too much to look up. She must now take leave of her queer companion. And who knew what would happen next ?

But her husband was not even thinking of them.  He was peering about on the grass, as careless as if they were his children coming home from walking.  "I've found eight glow-worms, George," said he.  "I tried to read my book by the moon, and found that a fallacy; so then I thought of what poets recommend and lighted the page with glow-worms."

Helen laughed.

"Would a firefly give you light enough, I wonder?" asked George.

"None that I ever came across, my boy."

"Don't ladies in South America stick the poor fireflies in their wreaths, with pins, and wear them in the evening?" asked Helen.  She had got all her spirits back again.

" Only the cruel ones," said her husband.

George smiled faintly. " Shall I fetch you some pins, Mrs. Tresham ?" he said, half aloud.

" I'll stay," murmured the wife, " and talk to you, Charles. Oh ! no, the night air won't hurt me now ; let us walk about and look at the water."

George took the hint and wandered off to his room ; and then he chose a book and sat in his arm-chair, biting his fingers. He was unhappy ; but still after a lofty fashion. He read on for a long time, and then set to considering what was wrong with him. " Please row back quick, George." That was all she had to say to-night. Perhaps he had offended her by staying out so late ; she was vexed. Yet what a faultless person she was. " Oh ! I'm more wretched than ever I was. Soon I will love her," he said, shuddering once ; and then starting up. To love her ! For a short second what a divine prospect that seemed ! But then a Judge's voice resounded in his ears ; was he a criminal then already ? Clearly he called to mind who she was now, and who he was. He dared not even look into such a tangle of guilt and treachery as venturing to love her would mean. And so it must be choked and put away from him at once. Here was a wife and a mother, two most holy names. And the bearer —was she not most sacred in George's eyes. Peace to his writhing! All this had come of his dreamy, idle life of late. The wild fancies he harboured at times frightened even himself. But this was worse than common madness. "I consume the night in idle guesses, while she, unconscious of my existence, at this time sleeps.—Where?" Sitting in his chair, George shuddered a little. But here now — he was once more raving, simply. He need not seriously debate those questions. Stealing fire from Heaven was never likely to be charged to him. As likely this; and so he silenced himself for a while, remaining there with the book on his knees. He read a page or two. "What was that last bit? my thoughts were off somewhere. Didn't her face look altogether different by the moonlight! How wonderfully her hair was arranged; a new way to-night. New, I am sure. . . Oh! I love her," he said, aloud. And the sound of his own hardened words seemed to profane the tranquil room.

"I love her far more than my life. Who else have I ever loved in this world?—who else?" But let it be so; she should never, never know it. He began to feel now that he must go away at once from Norton. The thought of that made him cold, and for a while he had no more strength. "If I was going away," he said, feebly, "I would ask to kiss her once upon the forehead, just at the last. And then say good-bye for always." And yet he had been so happy here. Seldom had he known what that was in all his life. Must he leave her and go and be miserable again? Not just yet, surely. Conscience should not be so hard on him! He would not love her, he promised to himself; but he might see her still. And turning this idea over and over and upside down often, in his head, he at last, bending his arm behind his head, fell asleep with a frown upon his face. In dreams he was back once more at Sawtry with Stephen and Traylen, hunting for rabbits in the park. They wandered up the domain wall till they lost their path, and came to a river, which wound far and away into the sky. And soon he awoke. The morning wind was moving the curtains gently; it was just the grew of dawn. "I cannot go away," he said.  "No; there is no need."

And then he went to bed, to sleep and forget as long as he could.

END OF VOL. I.

T. C. Newby, 30, Welbeck Street, Cavendish Square, London.